Francis King spent his c
was a government official
he wrote his first three n........ .... joined the British
Council, working successively in Italy, Greece, Egypt, Finland and Japan, before retiring in 1964 to devote himself entirely to writing. His recent books have included the novels *The Action, Voices in an Empty Room* (Penguin, 1985) and *Act of Darkness* (Penguin 1985), chosen by the *Yorkshire Post* as Novel of the Year, 1983; two highly praised volumes of short stories, *Hard Feelings* and *Indirect Method*; and two non-fiction works, *E. M. Forster and His World* and *Florence*. For some years he has been Drama Critic of the *Sunday Telegraph* and he reviews fiction regularly for the *Spectator*. He is a former winner of the Somerset Maugham Prize and the Katherine Mansfield Short Story Prize. He has also edited and introduced *Writings from Japan* by Lafcadio Hearn, published in the Penguin Travel Library.

Francis King has been active on behalf of writers. A founder member of Writers' Action Group, which was involved in the final battle for Public Lending Right (PLR), he is President of English PEN.

FRANCIS KING

* * *

THE NEEDLE

PENGUIN BOOKS

Penguin Books Ltd, Harmondsworth, Middlesex, England
Viking Penguin Inc., 40 West 23rd Street, New York, New York 10010, U.S.A.
Penguin Books Australia Ltd, Ringwood, Victoria, Australia
Penguin Books Canada Limited, 2801 John Street, Markham, Ontario, Canada L3R 1B4
Penguin Books (N.Z.) Ltd, 182–190 Wairau Road, Auckland 10, New Zealand

First published by Hutchinson Books 1975
Published in Penguin Books 1986

Made and printed in Great Britain by
Richard Clay (The Chaucer Press) Ltd,
Bungay, Suffolk
Filmset in Monophoto Plantin Light by
Northumberland Press Ltd, Gateshead,
Tyne and Wear

To Sylvia

I

Like strangers thrown together fortuitously at the same table in an overcrowded café and determined not to be invaded by each other's identities, brother and sister breakfasted in the dark, high-ceilinged, old-fashioned kitchen above the surgery. From time to time Lorna would say 'Oh God, this room is so depressing!' and Bob would then reply that all it needed was a quick going-over with some paint. The paint had been bought, three tins of it were gradually gathering dust in the cupboard under the stairs; and on the promise of that quick going-over Lorna had got into the habit of hurriedly scribbling down on the blotched wallpaper above the telephone the names and addresses of patients who rang up while she was in the kitchen. But somehow, like so much else that Bob promised, the job never actually got done.

Bob raised his eyes from *The Times* as an umbrella bobbed past the window to a clatter of heels descending to the basement.

'Mrs E.,' he said.

'Yes, Mrs E.,' his sister sighed, reaching out for the percolator with a hand made ugly by chilblains. She was very conscious of those chilblains, because she knew that her patients were conscious of them. 'That means five minutes.'

Bob looked at his watch. It was an expensive one, given to him by Lorna on the first of his birthdays that they had spent together after he had returned, three years previously, from Kuala Lumpur, as mysteriously bereft of most of his possessions as of will. 'Seven,' he corrected. 'Something must be wrong with her.'

Another umbrella passed the window; these feet moved cautiously from one slippery iron step to the next. Then a youth clattered down, nose aflame and barking like a dog into the handkerchief that he held to his mouth.

'There'll be a lot of them today.'

'And how you really hate them!'

'Don't be silly.' Lorna rose heavily to her feet, twisting her napkin into the ring that had once belonged to Dada, their stepfather. But she wondered, uneasily, if he might not be right. Perhaps she had now come to hate them, as inexplicably as, for a brief period after the death of her elderly husband, Alfred, also a G.P., she had come to love them.

'Before you go – do get hold of your diary.'

'Oh, not *now*!'

'But I've no idea – absolutely no idea – what you're doing all this week.'

'My diary's in the bedroom.'

'Well, get it! Get it! It won't take a minute. And the patients will be perfectly happy chatting to each other about their bunions and perforated appendixes and external and internal piles even if you *are* late for them.'

'That's Matty's car.' Lorna peered out of the window at the bug-like three-wheeler from which her partner was struggling to extricate herself. She never allowed anyone to go to her assistance, even when one of her crutches slipped from her grasp to the road; but though Lorna had known this for many years, each time that she saw the twisted body emerging from that jaunty carapace she always had to conquer the desire to run out and call 'Wait! Let me help you! Let me help you!'

'On time for once!' Bob and Matty neither liked nor approved of each other; and for that reason Matty, once such a frequent visitor to the house from the surgery, was now seldom seen upstairs. 'Oh, do stay and have some supper with us,' Lorna would say after evening surgery; but Matty would shake her head of close-cropped, grey, wiry hair as she swayed on her crutches to the door:

'Sweet of you, pet. Another time. Not this evening. I've so much to do.'

'A drink then.'

'No, pet. Honestly. You know how it is.'

Yes, Lorna knew how it was.

8

'It must be a terrible struggle for her just to get a day started,' Lorna mused.

'She's got that adoring mother to help her, hasn't she?'

'An adoring mother of eighty-three.'

'The diary,' he reminded her. 'Quick.'

Lorna fetched the diary. Breathless from her climb up the stairs, she began to flick over the pages to the week ahead of them.

'Well?'

'Tomorrow's the day I invited the Thurstons in to dinner. Remember?'

'Oh, I can do without them.' Bob, who had now lit a cigarette, flicked some ash into the saucer of his coffee-cup. 'I'll be out.'

'But you know how keen Miranda is to see you . . .'

'Yes, I know. I know only too well. But – I'll be out.' As Lorna gazed desolately at the diary, her lower lip caught between her teeth, he jumped up and she felt the silk of his dressing-gown along her forearm and his hand on the nape of her neck, pinching it, as he so often did, in a manner as much punitive as playful. 'Oh, she'll be disappointed – of course she will – but *he'll* be glad. And you'll be able to have a nice cosy little chat, the three of you, about the difficulties of coping with your respective brats.'

'We do talk about other things, you know.'

'Sometimes.' He released her. 'But usually it's their darling Pat and Derek and your darling Edie. Isn't it?'

'And what'll you do?'

'I? Oh, I'll amuse myself in some way or other. You don't have to worry about me. You know that. Now what else?'

'Oh, Bob, I really must –'

'Quick!'

'Well, there's nothing else planned except that concert at the Festival Hall. André Previn. *Belshazzar's Feast.* Friday. You said you might like to come too.'

'Did I? I must have been crazy. No, no André Previn and no *Belshazzar's Feast.* I hate the vulgarity of both. So that's Tuesday and Friday you've got booked up?'

'So far. Yes. But you know, Bob, just because *I* happen to have nothing on one evening, that doesn't mean that *you* have to – '

9

'But it's more convenient if I go out when you have something else to do or someone else to see and if I'm in when you're on your own. Isn't it?'

'I suppose so.'

'So that's it. I'll take myself off on Tuesday and Friday.' He eased the diary out of her hands, closed it and then handed it back to her. 'And now you'd better take yourself off to those patients of yours.'

She slipped the diary into a pocket as he crossed the kitchen to the sink, turned on the hot tap and began to hold first one hand and then the other under the water. Each hand in turn went limp, the fingers dangling loosely. He made no effort actually to wash them; he did not take up the soap.

Lorna watched him for several seconds. This ritual, so often repeated, water cold or hot trickling over hands that seemed to have become suddenly nerveless, always fascinated and sometimes even frightened her. Once, she had asked him:

'Why do you do that?'

'Do what?' He had been standing at her wash-basin in her hotel room in Madrid, where the two of them were holidaying.

'Keep washing your hands.'

'I like them to be clean.'

'But they are clean. Already.'

'Then I suppose that the psychiatrists would say that I was trying to wash away some guilt.'

'Guilt! Have you any guilt?'

'I didn't say that. I said that that's what the psychiatrists would say.' He had looked mockingly at her, as he reached for her towel to dry each hand with the scrupulousness of an experienced butler polishing glasses.

'Run along!' Now, too, he was looking at her with the same mocking gaze, easing the cuticles back from one finger after another with the towel he had whipped off its peg. 'Don't keep them waiting! Matty's the one who's usually late. Not you. Remember?'

2

A moist film began slowly to well over the pale blue eyes and then a tear shuddered, impaled on one of the improbably spiky eyelashes, and finally disintegrated on to a high cheekbone hectic with rouge.

'I suppose it's my time of life.'

'Well, partly, of course.'

Partly, yes. But mostly that grey shape, a magnified grub, that this trembling, tearful woman had tended with so much care and love for – what? – four, five years.

'Sometimes I just can't stop myself crying. There's no reason for it.' (No reason but the grub, incontinent, almost motionless, silent but for those sporadic, wild, unintelligible yelps. Unintelligible to everyone but her, the interpreter of them.) 'None at all.' A hand, nails scarlet, jerked a handkerchief from the bag on her bony knees, to press it first to lips and then to the line of the jawbone, as though at a sudden stab of toothache. 'We've had our Nanette staying with us for the last ten days, so that ought to have cheered me up. Specially as she's always so good with him, not like her sister. But suddenly I find myself crying and there's no reason, no real reason, for it. Except, I suppose, my time of life.'

'I'll give you some pills,' Lorna said, drawing a prescription pad towards her. It was easier to write on a form than to struggle to say words of consolation or encouragement. Matty would not have to struggle to say them; they would come of their own accord. That, of course, was why most of the patients preferred to be seen by Matty, even though she had none of Lorna's diagnostic flair.

'Pills? But I'm quite well in myself, Dr Martin. It's just this thing of not, well, not somehow . . .'

'These pills are what we call anti-depressants. They cheer you up.'

'Well, I need that.' A doubtful smile.

'What you do is take one of them on the first night – tonight. Then two of them the next night. Three of them the night after that. And so on, until you reach five.'

'Five! Isn't that an awful lot?'

'No. Each of these pills is of a very small quantity.'

'A very small quantity,' the woman repeated, staring at the prescription pad on which Lorna was still writing.

'Now,' Lorna went on, 'if you find in the morning that you are having unpleasant side-effects, well, don't increase the dose in the evening, just stop there.'

'Side-effects?'

'I'll tell you what they might be. Firstly, drowsiness.' The woman nodded. 'Then dryness of the mouth. Thirdly, constipation.'

'Oh, I've never had that in my life! Never! If anything, it's always been the opposite.'

'Well, it could happen and if it does you must take something for it, that's all.'

'Something like senna? Paraffin?'

Lorna nodded. 'Lastly – not many patients experience this and, not having experienced it myself, I can't describe it – but there can be a strange feeling of, well, disassociation.'

The woman frowned, ventured on the first two syllables of the word, 'Disass –', and then gave up with a sigh.

'I gather it's rather unpleasant. You feel you're not in contact with the world around you. You're outside it all. One of my patients said it was as if there were a glass wall between her and everyone and everything else.'

The woman shook her head, bewildered.

'Anyway, it's highly unlikely that you'll get that kind of reaction. But if you do – well, come and see me again and we'll think of something else.'

'Do you think I really need these pills? As I said, in myself I'm really quite fit. It's just that –'

'Yes, I think you do need them. Please try them. They'll also help you to sleep.'

'I mustn't sleep too heavily. I've got to wake if he calls.'

'Oh, you'll do that all right.'

When Lorna saw out this last of her patients, Matty had already finished, writing at her desk as Mrs Emerson, one of two receptionists who also acted as cleaner, swept up around her with ill-tempered jabs of the broom.

'So that's that. Until this afternoon.'

'You look tired, pet.'

'How they drain one!'

'And half of them have nothing wrong with them that an aspirin or a teaspoonful of bicarb wouldn't put right,' Mrs Emerson sniffed, as she flicked her sweepings into a dust-pan. 'You're too patient with them by half. Both of you.'

Lorna shrugged and then began to take off her overall. Matty stared at Mrs Emerson's stooping back, hooded lids low over her small pale green eyes, as though in an effort to focus; then she gave herself a little shake and went on with her writing.

'I'll give your room a quick do round and then I'll be off,' Mrs Emerson said to Lorna. 'Got the old man at home with a nasty feverish cold. I can't come upstairs today.'

'It's going the rounds,' Lorna said, as she had already said to a number of her patients.

'He thinks I bring these germs back with me from here,' Mrs Emerson grunted, suddenly truculent.

Matty laughed. 'Oh, I hardly think that!'

Lorna sank sideways into the straight-backed chair over which Matty's patients usually draped their clothes, a hand to her forehead.

'You need a holiday.'

'Perhaps I do.' Mrs Emerson had left them and her departure had brought Lorna a sudden relief. There was no longer any need to keep up pretences; with Matty, there never was. 'That woman – that Mrs Page – oh *God* how she depresses me!'

'What was the matter with her? Or did she come about him?'

'No. About herself. For once. She makes me want to cry and she makes me want to – oh – kick her. At one and the same time. And both feelings are *awful*.'

'Why should you want to kick her?' Matty asked in a conversational tone of voice, as though there were nothing odd in such an impulse.

'Oh, I don't know, I don't know, Matty! But – well, no one has the right to be quite that noble. How *can* she bear to do it? Tending that – that vegetable day after day after day. She hardly ever leaves the house except to shop. And it's now, oh, at least four years since he had that stroke. And you know – and I know – and even she knows that he'll never get any better.'

'I suppose in a well-organized society' – Matty examined the tip of her pen, again with those hooded lids low over her small eyes – 'euthanasia would be the answer.' It was impossible to tell from her dry, matter-of-fact tone whether she was being ironical or not.

'Oh, somehow – somehow I can't accept that.' Lorna shrank into the chair as though from some physical threat.

'Well, what else *is* there? Either you must accept that alternative or you must accept the one of poor old Mrs Page spending years and years tending a vegetable.'

'There are homes.'

'Which means that other poor people have to tend the vegetable.' Matty put the top back on her pen, aligned it beside the blotter and then began to struggle to her feet. 'But I suppose' – she was breathing effortfully, knuckles white as they pushed her up off her chair with the desk-edge as their fulcrum – 'I'm really a very good argument against euthanasia. No one ever thought I'd walk again, let alone take up a job like this. But there you are. I managed it.'

Lorna hardly heard her, all at once absorbed in a private reverie of her own. Then she said: 'I suppose there *is* something heroic about Mrs Page. And if the old boy had been painlessly put to sleep or carted off to a home – well – that heroism would never have come to the surface. Would it?'

'I suppose not,' Matty said. 'I suppose that's the only way to explain all the horribleness of life. That it purges and purifies. But I've never really been able to buy that one.'

Lorna got to her feet with a sigh and followed Matty out into the hall that also served as a waiting-room.

'Why not come and have a bite with us?' she said. 'No need to make the journey home.'

'Oh, me old mum' – Matty frequently referred to her mother like this, in a stage-Cockney accent – 'is expecting me home for bangers and smash. She's not very imaginative about food, poor old dear.'

'How is she?'

'A marvel – a ruddy marvel.'

'Have a meal with us some other time. Will you?' A pleading, coaxing note had entered Lorna's voice.

'Of course, pet. Any time you ask me.'

'But I often ask you.'

'Ask me in advance, I mean.'

'Well, of course we'll do that.'

'How's Bob?'

'Bob? Oh, he's all right.'

'Found anything yet?'

'Well, he's still doing this film-extra stuff of his.'

'That's hardly a job, is it? Once a week, twice a week.'

'He's looking around.'

'He's been looking around for an awfully long time.'

'Oh, Matty! Don't have it in for him so! Please!'

'I don't have it in for him, pet. Not at all.' Matty remained calm, leaning against a wall, her crutches under her arms. 'But what does he find to *do* all the time? He can't be happy. Not really happy.'

Lorna thought for a moment. Then: 'I don't know. I just don't know. *Is* he happy? Perhaps he is. You and I have this puritan thing of never really being at ease with ourselves unless we're perpetually *doing* something. Well, he doesn't have that. A lot of young people don't, I find. There are other ways of finding salvation than through work.'

'Well, I hope he's on the way to finding it,' Matty commented drily, giving herself a push away from the wall and lurching towards the door. She turned. 'So what did you do for Mrs Page?'

'Mrs Page?' Lorna was momentarily bewildered by the change of subject.

'What was the matter with her?'

'Can't stop crying. Menopausal depression, I suppose – on top of everything else.'

'And so you prescribed – ?'

'Not the old boy's death – though that would probably be the most certain cure.'

'I'd not be sure of that.'

'I wrote her out a prescription. What else can one do?'

'A triptezol trip?'

'That's right.'

'Well, good luck to her. Some of my patients tell me that it makes you feel as if you were walking two feet off the ground. I wish I could feel like that sometimes!' She began to drag herself out into the area. 'Well, 'bye for now, pet!'

'And you won't forget that meal with us!' Lorna called after her.

'Not on your life!'

3

'Good God! After midnight. I'm afraid we've rather overstayed our welcome.'

'That was a super meal, love. Those *quenelles* were out of this world.'

They had, in fact, been out of a tin; but Lorna did not tell Miranda Thurston that.

'I'm glad you liked them.'

'This has been the kind of evening I really enjoy. Just the three of us, having a lovely natter.'

'Except that it would have been even more fun if Bob had been here too,' Brian took up.

'He asked me to give you his love. He had this – this other engagement. He tried to get out of it but couldn't.' It was odd that she could lie so effortlessly about things like the *quenelles* and yet should always be so transparently clumsy when lying about Bob.

'It's an age since we saw him.' Miranda suppressed a little shudder as she drew her mink stole closer about her. The Thurstons' vast flat in Bedford Walk was centrally heated to the temperature of a greenhouse and still she complained of draughts and feeling cold. Lorna's hall had only the grudging warmth of an oil stove, the reek of which often crept stealthily up the stairs and even into the bedrooms. 'How's he getting on?'

'Oh, fine. Fine.'

'What exactly is he doing now?' It was the question that Matty was always asking.

Lorna opened the front door in the hope that this would curtail the inquisition, murmuring:

'Oh, this film-work. You know. What he's always been doing.'

'Does it get him anywhere?' Brian asked.

Lorna shrugged. 'It makes him money. He had a small part in

one of these Frankie Howerd films. Up the something-or-other.'
The small part had been an unspeaking one.

'Well, that must have been fun,' Miranda said, shivering visibly now as she edged towards the door.

'Do tell him – if he'd ever like me to do anything . . . I mean, from time to time a vacancy comes up in the old firm . . .'

'That's awfully kind of you, Brian.'

Over Brian's shoulder and far up the street Lorna had caught a brief glimpse of Bob, appearing under a lamp-post and then hurriedly retreating.

'How this neighbourhood's gone up!' Miranda exclaimed, as she made her way cautiously down the steps, an arm linked with her husband's for support. Her heels were extremely high and above them her legs, so thin that one felt that a single jar would snap them, looked terribly vulnerable to Lorna. It was the first time that she had ever associated vulnerability with the woman who was, she supposed, her closest friend. 'Look at all those cars. Jags and a Bristol over there and – and, yes, even a Rolls!'

'Yes, I suppose Parson's Green has made it at last.' Lorna peered uneasily to see what had happened to Bob; but he had vanished from sight.

'Don't stay out in this cold. Lovely to have seen you. And thank you again.' Miranda pressed an icy cheek to Lorna's flushed one.

'Marvellous evening. You always do us proud.' Lorna smelled the expensive after-shave lotion as Brian's lips touched her fore-head.

Lorna went back into the house and shut the front door behind her. Then, arms crossed under her breasts and the oil stove scorching the backs of her legs, she stood and waited.

After two or three minutes Bob's key turned in the lock and the door swung open.

'Lorna! Still up? I imagined that you would have gone to bed long, long ago.'

'You imagined no such thing. You saw Brian and Miranda leaving.'

'Did I?'

'Of course you did. You saw them and ran away.'

Bob laughed and eventually she began to laugh with him.

'Somehow I couldn't face them. Not at this hour. What made them stay so late?'

'I suppose Miranda wanted to see you. That seems the most likely explanation.'

'Was the evening fun?'

'It was – all right.'

'Not really fun. But you managed to have what Miranda would call "a lovely natter", I expect?'

As always he knew it all.

Lorna sighed. 'Miranda depresses me so.'

'Depresses *you*? She makes *me* feel suicidal.'

'I can't keep up with her. All that elegance. No one would ever suppose that she and I had been to school together. She still looks *young*, Bob. Whereas I . . .'

'Poor darling.' He put his arm around her; and at that contact she was suddenly aware of a feverish warmth that was kindled in his glittering eyes and flushed cheeks and radiated from his body, as it stood so close to her own. He might have just been victor in some race or have stepped off a stage after receiving an ovation at the end of a long and exhausting performance. 'Of course she *looks* young. Because she does nothing else but keep herself young. But inside – oh, she's raddled and ancient.'

'What have you been doing?'

He ignored the question. 'Christ, I could do with a bite to eat!'

'Haven't you had any dinner?'

'Oh, that was an age ago. What have you got left from your feast?'

'Some *quenelles*. They won't make particularly appetizing left-overs. But there's some home-made tomato soup and some apple crumble and, oh, lots and lots of cheese. They didn't seem to want any.'

'I'll settle for some bread and cheese.'

As they went into the kitchen, Bob placed a hand on her shoulder and again she felt radiating from him, through this lightest of connections, a heat that spread uncomfortably over the surface of her body and up into her face. 'Oh, that cat!' he exclaimed,

19

removing the hand from her shoulder and waving it at Anna, the Siamese, who was crouched on the table among the stacks of unwashed crockery and cutlery from dinner. The cat flopped from the table and whisked between Lorna's legs and out into the hall.

'Don't!'

'But it's so insanitary – sitting among the things from which we eat. I don't know how you can bear it – and you a doctor.'

'The dish-washer sterilizes them'

'Does it?'

'Of course it does. You used to like cats once.'

'Still do.'

'You don't like Anna.'

'I like her in her place. And that's not on the beds or the chairs, much less the kitchen table.'

Lorna sighed. They had had this argument many times before.

'Camembert! And just right, too! Feel!' He held it out to her.

'I wonder why they didn't want any cheese. God knows what we'll do with it all. I'll have to give some to Matty or Mrs E.'

'You'll do no such thing. I'll eat it. You'll see.'

As he began to bite into a doorstep of French bread spread thick with Camembert, Lorna asked again: 'What have you been doing?'

'Doing? Nothing in particular . . . Be an angel and pour me out some of that claret left in that bottle.'

As she emptied the bottle into a glass, Lorna felt her whole body sag and ache with tiredness. Miranda and Brian usually had that effect on her: first the hectic exhilaration while they were present, then this overwhelming weariness of both flesh and spirit. 'Tell me,' she said.

'Tell you?' He swallowed; then wiped some crumbs off his bottom lip with the back of a hand. 'Tell you what?'

'How you spent the evening.'

'But there's nothing *to* tell.'

'I'd like to know, none the less. Why don't you ever *talk* to me, Bob?'

'Talk to you! What *do* you mean? I'm always talking to you.'

'Never about yourself. Never.'

'Well, that's probably because I only like talking about things that are interesting.'

'You're interesting, aren't you? To me at any rate.'

He was silent, spreading Camembert on to another thick hunk of bread and then biting into it with those white, even teeth of his.

'Aren't you?'

'I don't know what you mean. I have no secrets from you.'

'Don't you? . . . Anyway, it's not a question of *secrets*.'

'Then of what?'

She hesitated a fraction. Then: 'Silence,' she said. 'I suppose. It doesn't matter if what you've been doing has been interesting or not. Just tell me. Tell me. I want to know.'

'Very well.' He smiled at her, elbows on the table as he held what was left of the slice of bread between both hands. The hands were thick and muscular in comparison with the rest of his body and he bit the nails methodically. People often remarked on the ugliness of those hands. They probably would not have done so if the rest of him were not so beautiful. 'I walked through Kensington Gardens just before it was closing and then I went for a drink to that place beside the Serpentine. The Pergola, is it? And then I looked in at two or three pubs and went to that posh new cinema in Knightsbridge, where I saw *High Society*. You remember that film?' Lorna nodded. 'We saw it together in Bournemouth, oh, years and years ago. We liked it then. I didn't like it this time round. Not at all.' He peered into his empty glass. 'I wish there were some more of that wine.'

'I can open another bottle.'

'Not worth while. Forget it.' He got up and began to run some water into the glass. His back to her as he stood at the sink, he said: 'Not very interesting, right?'

'You haven't got the point.'

'What is the point?'

'There's this lack of communication. It worries me.'

He turned round; he was no longer smiling with that old indulgence. 'There's no lack of communication between us. No more than between any two human beings. People *are* separate.

They can only know so much about each other. So much and no more.'

'But I know so little.'

'You know everything that's of any importance.'

'Do I?'

'Of course you do.'

'I did once. No longer. No longer, Bob.'

'Once! Oh, once!'

4

Once Lorna had lived in this same house, large and even then ramshackle, with an adored father, a doctor who practised homoeopathy when homoeopathy was no longer fashionable and an invalid mother whose medicine bottles glinted in serried ranks from the bedside table of the shadowed bedroom that she now shared only with the demons of migraine, bilious attacks and nerves. There had been an influenza epidemic and the mother had taken once more to the bed from which she had risen two days previously, complaining of a swimming sensation in her head and an increasing huskiness, while the husband had gone out on his rounds late into the foggy evening, his face oddly smudged – Lorna always remembered that, wondering if it had really been so or if she had imagined it so – as she had helped him on with his coat in the hall in which, even then, a paraffin stove, not the present one but one that stank even more strongly, flickered its blue tongue. He had come back on a stretcher, carried out from an ambulance one door of which, hanging loosely open, had creaked back and forth in the icy wind. Some virus had attacked his heart, they were later told after his death the following evening. His wife was, unaccountably, pregnant, but she had not known that at that time.

Three years later she married one of the two doctors who had taken over the practice. By then the migraines, bilious attacks and nerves had become, mysteriously, things that had afflicted someone else. There was no longer a wan, querulous woman wandering around the house or resting on a bed or sofa, but a brisk, domineering housewife, the colour of her cheeks unusually high and the tone of her voice unusually peremptory. She looked after the baby, as she looked after the house and the garden, capably but with no affection. Her only affection was for her second husband, who had never married until his forty-fourth year, who took pride in some tenuous aristocratic connections and who could never bear to look at his patients directly in the eye or to speak to even the deafest of them in more than a mumble. He wore the cleanest and finest of linen and in the vast compactum that still stood, empty now, on the upstairs landing, there had been ranks of suits, all dark in tone, and rows and rows of ties. He smelled vaguely of lavender and his hair, blond and silky, was worn unusually long for that period just after the war.

He never seemed at ease with his wife who cosseted and coaxed and occasionally bullied him as a nanny, kindly but firm, bullies a wayward and over-imaginative child. Nor did he seem at ease with his patients; with the friends, all male, with whom he would play chamber music two and three evenings each week, tucking his viola under his small, pointed chin, while his hair fell across his forehead in malleable fronds; or with his partner, Alfred, the genial widower, almost ten years older than himself, whom Lorna was finally to marry. Only with Lorna, then eight years old, did his tremulous nerves steady themselves, his melting, shifting gaze focus and become direct, his voice cease to slur and hesitate; and she, bereft of the once ever-loving, now ever-mourned father who had failed even to acknowledge her when she had leant over his twisted, congested face on the stretcher, had responded to him half in embarrassment and half in love.

This stepfather, she knew now, had always hated Bob, however hard in the early years he had striven to persuade others and, more important, himself that he did not do so. There had been the period of infancy, some three or four years, when he had been foolishly indulgent, like some maiden aunt, secretly discountenanced, clucking and cooing. Then for another period, some five years this time, he had grown increasingly remote, the long-lashed eyes becoming even more unfocused and the always evanescent thread of the voice becoming so thin that it all but disappeared entirely whenever circumstance obliged him to look at or speak to this beautiful, talented, affectionate child whose existence he would have liked to erase as sharply, cleanly and decisively as he erased the blond, wispy moustache that he had once mysteriously

24

grown for a few weeks and then no less mysteriously, had removed one morning with the cut-throat razor that always terrified Lorna when she peeped into its box. Lastly there had come the period, dragging on and on until his premature death, a greying wraith, from cancer of the pancreas (how he had come to hate the sweet things, the cakes from the Belgian patisserie, the thimblefuls of liqueurs after dinner, the chocolates and sweets that previously he had loved so greedily), when he could only speak to the boy with an icy sarcasm and could only bear to glance at him with contempt.

What an extraordinary imagination that child had! The genial, himself unimaginative widower whom Lorna had married, never ceased to marvel at it. *Where does he get it from? How does he think of these things? One day he'll become a literary man of some sort, you mark my words. A novelist or a dramatist or something of that kind.* Strange and marvellous things were always happening to the boy, when he was seven, eight, nine, ten; but whether they were happening in reality or in his own mind, no one, least of all Lorna, ever knew exactly. *Oh, you do tell fibs! It* COULDN'T *have been like that! I don't believe that anything like that ever took place at all! I don't believe that such a person ever existed!* But, so literal-minded herself, she was enchanted and enthralled.

Their stepfather, however, would unravel each story with sour, sardonic persistence. Here were a few threads of facts, and here was a whole mass of what he did not call, as others might, fantasy or exaggeration but, quite simply and brutally, lies, lies, lies. *So, tell us, my dear boy* (he lingered over the 'my' and the 'dear' to give them meanings the exact opposites of their usual ones) *where did this rather bizarre experience come to you? Oh, in Cullen's, was it? When you went to buy your mother some castor sugar? And how – do explain to us – was a woman with five Pekineses in Cullen's? It seems a trifle odd. Because, you see, dogs are not allowed in Cullen's. They're not allowed in a number of grocers' shops. For reasons of hygiene. They're not allowed in Cullen's.* And so eventually the weird, astonishing stories of fortuitous witnessings of a woman surrounded by a multitude of Pekineses, of bank hold-ups, of bodies being dragged green and swollen out of the Serpentine, of car-crashes and fights between drunken Irish labourers and dark foreigners lurking mysteriously at the bottom of the garden came to be told only to Lorna. Still she would cry out in protest – *Oh, you do tell fibs! Honestly! Really!* But she always listened to him with wonder and a deep, barely acknowledged love.

Then the time came when he was sent away to boarding-school. *It's ghastly, the cost of it. We'll have all of us to retrench all round. But it's the best thing for the boy, the only thing. He needs the discipline.* (There had never been any discipline in the stepfather's own weakly disordered life.) *Put an end to all this idiotic romancing. Give him a sense of reality. Teach him what's what.*

Bob had returned for the summer holidays a bare three months later, remote and self-possessed. He and Lorna still spent much of their time together, despite the seven-year difference in their ages (a precocious seventeen, she was just about to go to Cambridge to study medicine), but though he chattered away to her, as he had always done, bright-eyed and eager, now it was all facts, facts, facts. He read a great deal and what he read he never forgot. But Lorna knew that, in some way he would never explain to her, school had inflicted a final, irreparable wound.

Oh, you never tell me stories now!
Stories? What stories? Oh, those!
You told me such marvellous stories once.
Once! Oh, once!

5

When the dish-washer had been loaded and the pans scrubbed out – Bob had not offered to help her – and Lorna was then at last dragging herself up the stairs to bed, she heard him call out to her through his half-open door: 'Oh, Lorna! Lorna!' his voice fretful, almost tear-laden, like a child's.

'Yes?' She halted on the landing, not entering the room or even pushing the door any further open, as she was swept by one of those inexplicable waves of exasperation against him that from time to time engulfed her. Oh, it was fair enough to go off leaving her with those mounds of plates and stacks of knives and forks from a dinner-party he had not, after all, attended himself, but at least he might have wrapped up the Camembert and put it away and thrown that orange-peel into the dustbin. 'What is it?'

'Give us a hand.'

'What with?' But she did not have to be told.

'Somehow this is one of those nights I just can't face it. It's such a revolting performance at the best of times. If you knew how it disgusted me!'

Reluctantly Lorna pushed the door open and stepped into the room. As always on these occasions, Bob sat slouched forward on the edge of his bed, the syringe in his hand and his trousers lowered to his knees.

'It's odd you've never really got used to it. After all these years. I've had so many patients who've told me that they'll never learn to do it and then after two or three weeks it's no more difficult for them than cleaning their teeth.'

'Or wiping their arses. Yes, I know, I know. You've told me that. I'm sorry. I wish I *could* get used to it.' He was now balancing the syringe on the palm of his hand, staring down at it with a distaste that seemed as much for himself as for it. 'I suppose I'm a coward. Dada was right.'

He must have been sitting there for a long time, trying to steel himself to plunge the needle into his thigh. The bare flesh above the lowered trousers was bluish and goose-pimpled.

'Give it to me,' she said, feeling a sudden remorse for her previous exasperation. But, strangely, he hesitated now. 'Come,' she said, holding out a hand. 'I don't mind. I'm doing this all the time. You know that.'

'It seems rather hard that you should have to do it at home too.' He gave a short, edgy laugh; then he held out the syringe to her, still balanced on a palm that was, she now saw, glistening with sweat despite those goose-pimples.

'Where do you want it?'

'Well, since you can reach behind and I can't, let's have it there.' With a small groan he rolled away from her and over, lifting the tail of his shirt with one hand while the other covered his mouth as though to stifle a possible scream.

'About here?'

Between the parted legs, she could see a wrinkled section of his scrotum. She pinched the flesh between forefinger and thumb.

He grunted.

'Cotton-wool?'

'Oh, don't bother about that.'

'Thank God for disposable syringes.'

'In K.L., you know ... I had this ... this servant ... this boy ...' He broke off with a little whimper, barely audible, as she plunged the needle home. She had heard before, many times, about this boy. 'He was a marvel at injecting me, a bloody marvel.' He was getting to his feet, pulling up his trousers, fumbling at the waist-band. 'One never felt a thing.'

'But you feel it when I do it for you?'

'Don't be silly! My God, you're not offended, are you? One expects a doctor not to hurt one. But in the case of an illiterate peasant boy not yet out of his teens ...'

'When did you last do a urine test?'

'Oh, a day or two ago.'

'Truthfully?'

'Of course! Why not?'

'Because you're so slack about them. If you want me to do one tomorrow . . .'

'You've more than enough on your plate. I know the drill.' He went towards her as she turned from dropping the syringe in the waste-paper basket beside his desk, and, smiling with an extraordinary, winning sweetness, put out his hands and placed them on her shoulders. 'Thanks, Lorna. I don't know why it should be but sometimes . . .' He gave a little shudder. 'It's one's *own* flesh. I think I could do it for you, for anyone else for that matter. But one's own flesh . . . You can understand that, can't you?'

'Of course I can.'

'Yes, of course you can. You can understand everything. That's what's so terrific about you.' His face came close to hers, closer and closer, as though he were examining every pore and line on it. 'You look done in.'

'I feel done in.'

'You shouldn't give these dinner-parties. Not after a long day of work.'

'One has to ask one's friends back.'

'Does it have to be a cutlet for a cutlet? Wouldn't drinks or coffee be enough?'

'Not for Miranda and Brian. You know how lavishly they always entertain us.'

'Well, Miranda has that woman she calls her "treasure". You only have Ma Emerson.'

'She's a treasure too in her way.'

He laughed. Again his face came closer and closer to her own, the amusement fading now and his expression growing distant, even stern. 'You do too much. For everyone.'

'I *have* to be busy. You don't understand that.'

'*Have* to be? That makes it sound as if you were – were terribly unhappy.'

'Not terribly. Perhaps not unhappy at all.' She could no longer meet his gaze. 'But with Alfred gone . . . and Edie no longer needing me much – or perhaps caring much about me . . .' She shrugged.

'Others need you.'

'Perhaps.'

'*I* need you.'

At that, she felt a sudden, panicky embarrassment. 'Well, I suppose I'd better turn in. Otherwise I'll be in no state for surgery tomorrow.'

'Thank you, Lorna.' He took her left hand in his right, pressing her fingers with his own so hard that it was almost as though he wished to hurt her. 'Thanks a lot.'

'Good night, Bob.'

'Good night. Sleep well. Happy dreams.'

It was what he had always said to her as a child; it was what he often still said to her when they turned in.

6

Lorna closed the door of her room, unscrewed her earrings and put them away in their box, and then sank onto the edge of her bed, in exactly the same slouched posture as she had found her brother. She shivered, though the room was warm from the gas fire she had lit before starting the washing-up, hugging herself as she did so.

'He'll have to learn!' Dada's voice was shrilly petulant. 'I forbid you to do it for him! It's not a kindness, it's honestly not a kindness. How's he going to manage in the years ahead? You can't always be around to stick a needle into him, you know.'

But at that period, a gauche, over-plump medical student who had never had a boy-friend, she had always secretly assumed that she would never cease to be around.

'But it's so awful for him. He really *dreads* having to do it.'

'Only now. It's just a question of getting used to it.'

Secretly she would often slip into Bob's room, while downstairs their mother and stepfather listened to the wireless, and would take the syringe from his nerveless fingers. 'I'll do it. Let me. Come on.'

'But I've got to learn. He says I've got to learn.'

'You will. Bit by bit. But I'll do it now.'

From this dependence she derived a secret, shameful thrill; and the shame was not only for disobeying Dada.

She remembered the first time that Dada had caught her at the actual moment of injection. He must have guessed what she had been doing, night after night, and he had crept up the stairs, the news still reverberating from the sitting-room, making not a sound, until he had flung back the door on the girl stooping, syringe in hand, over the boy, whose face was buried in his pillow.

'What *is* this? What *are* you doing? What did I tell you?'

Her only answer had been to plunge the needle home at the same moment that, roused by the voice, Bob had begun to squirm round.

'The boy's a coward. But there's no point in encouraging his cowardice. Don't you see that?' His pointed chin was tilted high and the nostrils of his bony nose were flaring. 'It's no kindness to him. He's got to learn. He's simply *got* to learn. Now go to your room.'

Lorna had gone.

She did not know what Dada had then said to Bob, but it was several minutes before there had been a knock at her door. 'One minute!' she called, slipping into an icy dressing-gown.

'I don't want you to do that again. Ever again. Do you understand?'

She hung her head; did not answer.

'Lorna!'

Still she did not answer.

'Did you hear me, Lorna?'

She raised her eyes at last; she stared at him with defiance. 'I can't undertake that. I can't make any promises.'

'Lorna! Lorna!' he chided her, his voice now soft and wooing. 'Why do you have to take this kind of attitude with me? I'm only trying to do what's best for him – and you. You sometimes make me think that you regard me as some kind of enemy – an interloper.'

'No, I don't do that. Of course I don't. But I wish ...'

'Yes?'

'Well, I wish you'd leave Bob alone!'

'I'm responsible for him, Lorna,' he reminded her in that same soft, wooing voice. She had heard him use it to some of his elderly female patients – not the working-class ones, as a rule – and he often used it to her. 'He needs a father – whether he likes it or not – and that's the role I've been cast to play for him. Unfortunately ... Don't be angry with me, Lorna.' His head was on one side now, the tip of his tongue between his full, soft lips and one eyebrow arched coquettishly. 'We've always been good friends. I only wish ... Oh, if only Bob weren't *quite* so difficult!'

'You're not exactly nice to him. Ever.'

'I do my best.'

'Oh, yes. Yes.'

'My goodness! How sarcastic we sound!'

'I don't mean to sound sarcastic,' she relented.

'Bob's not easy. You don't seem to realize that. He's a clever boy and in many ways he's a *good* boy. But he's also – odd, rather odd.'

'*Odd?*'

'I think that his real father dying like that before he was born . . . It's had a far worse effect on him than he's ever let on. I know you think I'm too hard on him – unfair to him – but his school reports . . .'

'I must get to bed,' she said on a sigh; and genuinely she had all at once felt an overmastering weariness, a desire to tumble, unwashed, into the bed, to pull the blankets over her head and to achieve an instantaneous, deep oblivion . . .

As she did now.

But when, shivering, legs drawn up and arms crossed under her breasts, she waited for sleep to come, her mind, a mole burrowing deeper and deeper into the darkness of the past, refused to be stilled. One image, seemingly totally unimportant and irrelevant, kept recurring among all the others. It was of Dada's frail, bony wrists shooting cuffs that were as immaculately white and stiff as those of a hospital matron, and below them those narrow, blue-veined hands with the nails that he buffed until they looked as if he had lacquered them.

7

'So it's rather a problem,' Edie sighed, picking with the nail of a forefinger at another almond on top of the Dundee cake. She began to munch.

'I wish you wouldn't do that.' Lorna knew at once that she should not have said it.

'Does it matter? Do you always have to fuss? You weren't like that once, you know.'

'Yes, I'm sorry. But it does make the cake look rather horrid for anyone else who comes.'

'*Is* anyone coming?'

'Well, Bob ought to be home eventually. And in any case, there's tomorrow, isn't there?'

'Do you want me to buy you some almonds and stick them back?'

'Don't be silly, darling! As you say, it doesn't really matter.'

'Then why behave as though it did?'

Lorna sipped her lukewarm tea. She had neglected it while making suitably sympathetic noises during Edie's narration of a whole sequence of troubles – with her boy-friend, with the two other girls who shared the flat with them, with the landlord, with an elderly neighbour – that had befallen her since her last weekly visit the previous Sunday. 'You could always come back here, darling.'

'*Here?*' Lorna might have suggested that Edie could camp out on the Green.

'Why not? You could lead your own life – cook for yourself if you wanted. We could get a little Belling boiler. Or we could even have a proper stove and a sink rigged up on the landing. Why not? It needn't cost too much. Matty has this little man – a Rumanian or a Hungarian – and when they divided off the house, he charged

34

her awfully little, hardly anything at all. Oh, it would be so lovely . . .'

But Edie was shaking her head as she picked at yet another almond on the cake. 'No, Mummy. Please!'

'But why not? Why not? It's the obvious thing. There's that whole top floor never used, and if you wanted to have Donald there too – I mean, if you patched things up again, as I'm sure you will – well, then, I shouldn't mind, I shouldn't mind a bit.

'No, Mother. No.' Edie began to nibble on the almond, holding it between forefinger and thumb, neither very clean, as her large green eyes squinted down at it.

She gets her looks from Bob, Lorna thought, as she had often thought before. Somehow it never ceased to be humiliating that her daughter had so obviously not got her looks from herself.

'I shouldn't interfere. Not at all. I know I've been, well, silly in the past. I admit that and I'm sorry for it. It's difficult for mothers to get used to the fact that their children are –'

'Oh, it's not *you*!' Edie interrupted crossly, dusting off the fingers that had held the almond on the side of her long, voluminous skirt. 'It's him.'

'Him?'

'Bob.'

'Bob wouldn't get in your way. Why should he? You needn't have anything to do with him at all – unless you want to.'

'Well, I don't want to.'

'When you were small you used to be so attached to him. Before he went away.'

'I wish he'd never come back, I really do!' She leant across the kitchen table for the teapot.

'What have you got against him?'

'Plenty!'

'But what? What?'

'I just don't like him. I just don't like him at all. And I certainly wouldn't come back to live in this house while he was here.'

'I can hardly put him out, darling.'

'I don't see why not.' Edie slurped noisily at her tea. 'Does he pay you?'

'He makes his contribution.'

'What does that mean?' Lorna did not answer, frowning down at her wedding-ring as her hands clutched the edge of the kitchen table. 'How much?' Edie pursued brutally.

'It's not a fixed sum.'

'I bet it isn't!

'When he does well, he's awfully generous.'

'Does he ever do well? How much can he earn in a week? I should think he averaged about twelve pounds a week – if that.'

Lorna wanted to cry out: Why are you so implacable about him? Have you forgotten how he used to take you to the playground and tell you bedtime stories and even bath you when I was late back from a patient? And how, later, he used to treat you to those visits to the theatre and how he accompanied you to that Billy Graham meeting, during that period when you 'got' religion, and how patiently and devotedly he nursed you through those long, debilitating months of glandular fever, fetching you your food and running errands for you and spending hours at your bedside?

But instead, since she was frightened of any show-down with her daughter, Lorna only said mildly: 'I wish you didn't have it in for him so.'

'I've told you. I just don't like him.'

'He's had a bad time. All his life he's had a bad time. You should try to understand that.'

'I don't see that his life has been so much worse than most people's.'

'Dada was beastly to him. And then – then in Malaysia . . . Well, something must have happened.'

'Something? What, for instance?'

'I don't know.' Lorna shrugged helplessly. Nor did she. 'But I have this sense . . . I can't explain it. Something went terribly wrong for him there, just as before – when he was teaching in Morocco – it all went right. But don't ask me what.'

'Doesn't he ever *talk* about it?'

'No. No, he doesn't. Except about this boy – this boy who worked for him. He used to give him his injections. He's told me that often. But that's nothing at all to do with it.'

'Did he leave Kuala Lumpur under a cloud?'

'I've no idea.'

'You must have *some* idea.'

Lorna had a very good idea that some cloud had existed; but as to its nature she could only speculate. She shook her head: 'None at all. But he came back from there . . . broken.'

'*Broken?*' Lorna was afraid that Edie was going to burst out laughing in incredulity.

'Yes. Broken.' And the simplicity with which Lorna repeated the word seemed suddenly to melt Edie's contempt and animosity.

'I wonder how – or why?' The girl's beautiful, serene face under the prongs of its unevenly cut blond fringe, now suddenly grew abstracted, saddened, darkened. 'Though I suppose one can guess.'

'Can one?'

'Well, of course!'

But the trouble was that Lorna could not guess. She did not wish to guess; and she would not now or at any time press Edie to guess for her.

Soon Edie was saying: 'Well, I suppose I ought to be going. This girl at the school says there may be a vacancy in the flat that she's sharing and I said I'd pop over to have a look.'

'Well, do bear in mind that *if* you should find –'

'Yes, Mummy. Yes.' Cruelly impatient.

But at the door Edie relented. She threw her arms round her mother. 'Poor Mother! Poor, poor Mother!'

'Why "poor", darling?' Lorna gave a little laugh but she felt like crying.

'Because you're so lonely – in spite of Bob and all those ghastly patients. And because I'm so beastly to you.'

'You're not beastly to me.'

'Yes, I am, I am! And I can't help it. That's the awful part. I just can't help it . . . Well, see you soon.' Suddenly she gave Lorna what was almost a rough push away from her.

'Your visits are always so short.'

'Now, Mummy! Please! Don't try to make me feel any more guilty than I do! Besides, won't Bob be home soon?'

'I've no idea. I suppose so.'

'Well, then!'

Lorna watched her daughter from the door as she swaggered off down the street in her high suède boots and her long suède coat. She tossed her head, ran a hand through her hair and then suddenly quickened her step. Lorna was prepared to wave to her if she looked back, as she sometimes did, from the corner. But Edie marched round it without a single backward glance.

8

'Damn!' Lorna jerked the two slices of charred bread from the defective pop-up toaster and then grabbed the telephone. She had overslept and, unless she hurried, would again be late for surgery. Bob, in pyjamas and dressing-gown, his soft blond hair neatly brushed and *The Times* propped up against the teapot in front of him, had paid no attention to either the acrid smell from the toaster or the insistent ringing behind him.

'Yes!' Probably it was yet another patient who had failed to notice that in the directory there were two numbers against Lorna's name – one marked 'surgery' and the other 'home'.

At some time, she could not remember when, she had heard the answering voice before; but whether in the flesh or, as now, over the telephone she could not be certain. 'Is Bob Ambler there?' The tone was impatient, even rude.

'Bob?'

Suddenly Lorna was aware that *The Times* was being waved at her, while, an anguished expression on his face, Bob shook his head vigorously from side to side.

'Bob Ambler. I want to speak to him.'

'He's just gone out.'

'Already? But he always tells me that he never goes out before eleven. I'm ringing earlier than usual.'

Earlier than usual? So presumably he was in the habit of ringing, no doubt after Lorna had already descended to the surgery.

'He had this appointment,' she lied. 'The dentist, I think. Shall I give him a message?'

There was a moment's hesitation. Then: 'Yes. Tell him to ring me just as soon as he gets in.' The caller might have been speaking to one junior employee about another junior employee. 'Tell him

I was expecting him last night and I want to know what the hell became of him!'

'What name shall I say?'

'Oh, he'll know who it is. Just ask him to ring me to explain what happened. Got it?'

'Yes. I'll see that –' Lorna began and then the telephone went dead.

She turned. Bob's mouth was slack; his hand gave a small twitch as it still held *The Times*.

'You heard that?'

'Part of it.' He made what seemed to be a conscious effort to steady both hand and voice, reached for his cup of tea and sipped. 'What was the trouble?'

'This man – he said you'd know who he was – wanted to know why you hadn't turned up last night, as expected.'

'Oh, to hell with him.'

As she began to cut some bread to replace the two charred slices she had flung into the dusbin, Lorna asked. 'Who was he?'

'Who?'

'That man. I've heard his voice before, I think. Have I met him? Or has he telephoned some other time?'

'You certainly haven't met him. You may have spoken to him on the phone some time or other.'

'Who is he?'

'Oh, an old bore. Someone from my days in K.L. A business-man.'

'And did you have a date with him? You did go out last night. And you did say you were going to meet a friend.'

'How you do keep tabs on me!' He gave a small, angry laugh. 'Yes, I met a friend. Not that friend. Another friend. If you really want to know, if it really interests you all that much. I'd half told that particular friend that I might, just might, look in to see him but then I couldn't face it.'

'You were back very late.'

'Precisely. I and the other friend had a lot of things to talk about. Do I have to account for my doings whenever I come home after midnight?'

'Of course not. Don't be silly.'

'After all, *you* went out. Didn't you?'

'To Matty. You could have come too.'

He sighed heavily, turning over a page of *The Times*. 'Yes, I suppose I could have done. But that would have been even more boring that an evening with the gentleman to whom you've just been talking.'

'Who is he? I didn't care for the way he spoke.'

'Oh. Why?'

'Well, he was so – so bloody brusque.'

'Perhaps he didn't realize who you were. Perhaps he thought you were the daily. Or perhaps he'd just got out of the wrong side of his bed this morning.'

'He spoke as though – as though he owned you.'

'*Owned* me? What are you talking about?'

'Well, employed you then. He spoke as though you were some employee who'd somehow let him down.'

'Don't be silly.'

'What's his name?'

'Don't be silly,' he repeated. 'Now eat your breakfast or you're going to keep all those lovely patients waiting. Come on! And watch that toast!'

As she munched the charred toast and gulped the scalding tea, Lorna thought, as she had often thought in the past: He tells me nothing. Or if he tells me something, it's somehow never the truth – or never the whole truth. He knows the names of all my friends and many of my patients. But of his friends I know nothing, nothing at all. Once I saw him from the car as he went into Harrods with that dark, foreign-looking man in the shimmering pale blue summer suit (could it have been he who telephoned?) and once I met him with those two other men, both obviously English, both red-faced and plump and balding, but he just said 'Oh, hello, Lorna!' and smiled and waved and passed on.

'Anyway, I've given you his message.'

'His message?' He looked up irritably from *The Times*; the whole conversation might never have taken place.

'To ring him back.'

'Oh, that! Well, I may get round to doing that some time or other. And again I may not.'

9

After twenty-two years she ought to have become sufficiently habituated not to suffer that involuntary rising of the gorge at the smells of fever, vomit and excretion in the sickrooms that she visited. Matty certainly had. 'Oh, I just no longer notice it,' she would say, reminding Lorna of one of her mother's friends, a wealthy, spoiled woman, long since dead, whose exquisitely furnished house in Eaton Square stank so revoltingly of the innumerable cats that whisked around it that even those closest to her found themselves making excuses to avoid her invitations. Yet she herself, beautifully groomed and gowned and so fastidious that she would have her maid take her pillows for her to any hotel in which she had to sleep, was totally unaware of the miasma in which she lived.

At the top of the area steps, her ankles still visible to the puffy old woman, an octogenarian Polish aristocrat who refused to abandon her dream of returning to the family's ancestral estates in what was now part of the Soviet Union, Lorna stood and drew in one deep breath after another, until her lungs began to ache from the strong, sharp air. Trucks hurtled past, vomiting their diesel fumes; but on the edge of that narrow pavement it was as if she was standing out on some promontory with a wind off the sea whirling all about her. The countess had tried to press on her some poppy-seed cake, a crumbling shortbread biscuit, a chocolate from a box that seemed to be filled with nothing but wrappings; but Lorna had known that if she had attempted to swallow anything at all, she would at once have spewed it out.

She pressed her handkerchief, smelling faintly of lavender, to her upper lip and continued to stare unseeingly into the traffic screeching and grinding past her, until she was aware that out on the green someone, seated on a bench with what looked like an outsize perambulator before her, was waving in her direction. It was the fur coat, with its high collar and its air of somehow simultaneously holding upright and holding together the skeletal figure within it (it could only have come from some jumble sale, Matty had once remarked), that made Lorna realize that, of course, it must be Mrs Page. And the giant perambulator . . .? She wanted to hurry off – that twenty minutes in the foetid basement with the Polish woman had been enough for her for the moment – but some compunction, some sudden access of pity or shame that took her by surprise, made her first wave back, the handkerchief already in her hand as though for that purpose, and then scuttle across the road in the face of a speeding Jaguar, the driver of which, a yellow-faced young man in a high-necked purple sweater (Lorna took it all in, in an instant) shouted something unintelligible but beginning C at her – cow, cunt, perhaps only 'Come *on*!' – as he simultaneously bleated his impatient fury on his horn.

'Hello, dear!' Mrs Page was surprisingly gay, almost saucy. She would never have called either Matty or Lorna 'dear' in the surgery; there each of them was always 'Doctor'. She patted the back of the bench with gloved hand as though in invitation. 'Been visiting?'

'Yes. I have a patient in the basement of the house on the corner.' Lorna simulated a shudder, not really feeling cold in the pale winter sunshine, and drew her old tweed coat closer about her. ('Honestly, you must do something about that awful garment!' Edie had said only that previous Sunday.) That way Mrs Page might not feel offended that she did not respond to the unspoken invitation of that gloved hand patting the back of the seat, while the other held the handle of the perambulator. 'I got frozen down there.'

'This sunshine's lovely, a real treat. That's why I brought him out. There's a patch of garden at our back but it never seems to get the sun – the factory shuts it out.'

Lorna had a moment of stunning realization. She peered under the hood. The grub lay there, motionless except for a tremor of the eyelids and a slight upward twist of one corner of his mouth (it looked like the snarl of a cornered animal but must have been

44

an attempt at a smile) as the washed-out pale blue eyes gazed back into her own. 'I knitted that blanket for him myself last winter,' Mrs Page was saying. 'It gave me something to do when I was sitting with him.'

'And the – the . . .' What should she call it? Carriage? Pram? Chair? Fortunately she did not have to formulate a word, since Mrs Page answered at once:

'It was Nanette's Oswald that made it. As a surprise. Three Sundays in a row he worked at it, Nanette told me. It makes me feel rather ashamed, to tell you the truth. I've said some hard things about Oswald in my time. But it's only his manner, I see now. At heart he's very kind really. You've not met him, have you?'

Lorna shook her head. The blanket had been knitted in red, white and blue squares that had then been unskilfully cobbled together. There was something terribly forlorn about it, as there was about the pram that must also have been cobbled together, admittedly with far more skill, from rusty bits and pieces of bicycles and invalid carriages and God knows what else.

'He doesn't like lady doctors, Oswald doesn't. That's why Nanette doesn't come to you any longer.' (Lorna and Matty had wondered about her defection.) 'He won't let her, see. So they both go to that Dr Simeon, you know who I mean.'

Again Lorna nodded, thrusting her hands yet deeper into the pockets of her coat and hunching her shoulders yet further.

'He's a great one for not prescribing medicines, Dr Simeon is. Let nature take her course is what he always says. Nanette had this upset tummy and he just told her not to eat and to let it all run out of her. That was the best way, he said.'

'Well, I suppose I'd better make my next call.' In fact there were no more calls to make. 'I had to park on the other side of the Green. It's murder trying to find a place.'

Mrs Page rose to her feet, tightening the knot of the crimson scarf that covered her head and then putting her hands on the bar of the perambulator. 'We might as well go home,' she said, not so much to Lorna as to the grub. 'You wouldn't want to miss *Waggoner's Walk*, would you? Would you now?' She said it in the

45

voice of a mother encouraging a fractious child. She turned to Lorna: 'It's funny how with certain programmes – not always the programmes that *I* favour, mind you – he suddenly comes alive. This *Waggoner's Walk* is one of them. You can *see* that he's taking it all in, even though, of course, he's got no way of showing it.'

'Can I help you?' Lorna asked, extending a hand to the perambulator.

'Well, that's very kind of you, dear.'

Strangely, the perambulator was hardly any weight at all. Lorna might have been pushing a trolley in a supermarket. 'It runs very smoothly,' she said.

'Yes,' Mrs Page agreed with pride. 'It has these wheels with air in them, see. Like a car. Well, they're really motor-bike wheels, that's what Oswald told me.' Their hands were touching now on the bar, the sleeve of Lorna's cloth coat from time to time brushing against the fur sleeve beside it. And then suddenly it came to her that Mrs Page had not really needed any help at all and that she had accepted the offer of it only out of some paradoxical kind of magnanimity – obviously it was a privilege to be allowed to help to push the grub.

'It's funny to think that he and his mates used to kick a football about over there during their midday break. That was less than, oh, five years ago.' Mrs Page jerked her head towards a bald patch of ground.

They had come to the pavement – gently, gently Mrs Page tipped up the perambulator from one level to the other – and now they waited as the traffic hurtled past them. 'The bastards,' Mrs Page muttered. 'You'd think one of them would stop.' Suddenly, so calm and bright before, she sounded on the verge of hysteria.

It was then that the extraordinary impulse came to Lorna; and the most extraordinary part of it was that, at the time, the impulse seemed to be totally ordinary. The perambulator was on the very edge of the pavement, blocking it with its length, so that passers-by, some resigned and some annoyed, had to step on to the Green in order to pass. The gloved hands rested lightly side by side. Eyes screwed together, a look of fury on her thin, hectic face, Mrs Page stared at driver after driver, willing one to stop. . . . It would

46

be so easy. A sudden, sharp push. The perambulator would tip down on to the road and shoot forward on those silent pneumatic wheels that Oswald had stripped off a motorbike. There would be a lorry like that one – as it thundered by, Lorna saw that it had a Spanish number-plate – or a Green Line bus like that one, with bored faces peering out through its windows, or even a Bentley like that one, though it would be a shame to damage and stain something so pristinely beautiful. Oh, it would be so easy; and the two of them would sob, ashen-faced, over the contents spilled from the perambulator and would explain how it had slipped, just slipped from their hands, each sure that it was the other who had a tight hold.

'Well, at last! So someone's got some Christian kindness after all. Of course it's a lady.'

An elderly woman had stopped her Mini for them and reluctantly the rest of the traffic beyond it halted too.

'Can I offer you a cup of tea?' Mrs Page suggested when they were at last on the other side. 'You look done in.'

'Oh, no. No, thank you. Really. I have this other patient still to see.'

'Well, it was a nice surprise, running into you like that . . . Oh, and I meant to tell you, I've felt ever so much better since you gave me those pills. My happiness pills, I call them.'

10

'Did you remember to ring up the agency?' Lorna reminded Bob when she came home that afternoon. Every day, at half past five, at six and then at six-thirty, he would make the calls. 'Robert Ambler,' he would say, and would then wait, an expression of exasperation on his face as he looked over at Lorna. Then he would usually mutter 'Thank you', shake his head and put down the receiver, saying, if it were one of the first two and not the last of his calls of that day, 'Well, I suppose something may possibly turn up later. Who knows?' On rare occasions, that in recent months had become rarer and rarer – there was a slump in the whole industry, he explained to Lorna, they just weren't making the huge blockbusters any longer – the procedure would be different and instead of the dispirited 'Thank you' he would scrabble about the telephone table for the piece of paper and the pencil or pen that he never seemed to have by him. Often he would write on the back of an envelope that Lorna had put out to take to the post, on a new magazine or on a prescription awaiting collection. 'Yes, yes … Pinewood … Fine … Fine … Yes, I'll be there …'

On this afternoon, as on a whole sequence of afternoons before it, he had been told there was nothing doing. Listlessly now, he played a game of patience, pondering the cards for seconds on end before he made a move.

'It all seems pretty hopeless. Why don't you try something else?'

'What else *is* there to try?'

'Hundreds of things.' There had been a time when Lorna, often of her own accord but also sometimes prompted by Matty, would underline in *The Times* an advertisement for this or that job: guiding foreign tourists, selling some product by telephone, helping in an antique shop. But such suggestions always made Bob either fretful or angry. 'It's a con, can't you see?' he would shout at her. Or: 'If you think that at my age I'm going to act as a glorified messenger-boy, you'd better think again!' Or: 'For Christ's sake let me get on with living my own life and get off my back!' So now, when Matty said that she had seen or heard of this or that job that seemed right, absolutely right for Bob – short hours, really not at all a bad wage – Lorna would at once silence her: 'It's not an atom of good, Matty. One must just leave him to get on with it by himself.'

'Or not get on with it,' Matty would then answer.

'Filming is something I enjoy doing.' Those ugly hands, so at variance with the beauty of the rest of his physique, hovered over the cards and then one descended, a nail scratched, the queen was moved under the king. 'For better or worse, it's my life, it's what I enjoy. And there's always still the chance that some day, some director ...' Yes, Lorna had heard on a number of occasions of how Zeffirelli had picked an unknown, hitherto unregarded extra to be his St Francis. 'It's a matter of luck.'

But you're not a lucky person, you never have been! It was what she wanted to cry out to him in mingled pity and anger, but of course she did not do so. 'Try again later,' she said. 'This is only your first call.'

'Yes, I'll do that. If you don't succeed at first, try, try, try again.'

When, after a cup of tea to warm her up and to take away that stale, sour taste of the Polish woman's den, lingering obstinately on the roof of her palate and the back of her teeth, Lorna clattered down the basement steps to the surgery – no sign of Matty yet and how forlorn the waiting-room looked through the window, with three patients, all middle-aged women, sitting as far apart as possible from each other, backs to the walls and out-of-date magazines on their laps! – she heard the telephone begin to ring out in the house above her. Well, no doubt Bob would interrupt his game of patience to answer it, though there were certainly times when he just did not bother, so that this or that patient would describe in an aggrieved voice how he or she had rung, oh, over and over again and there was just no one there.

After surgery Matty was obviously having what she herself would call her 'black dog'. The expression puzzled Lorna because, ardent dog-lovers, Matty and her mother kept an ancient and obese black poodle, which was sometimes even brought to the surgery, where it snored and snuffled contentedly under Matty's desk. When she was in one of these periodic states of quiet desperation Lorna knew better than to try to jolly her out of it or even to talk to her more than was absolutely essential. Eventually the black dog would slink away and Matty would become her usual gallant, sardonically cheerful self. It might be a matter of hours; it might, on the other hand, be a matter of days. The patients probably would not notice because to them she still kept up a front of jolly amiability, even though her eyes had about them a squinting, unfocused gaze and her lips, between the smiles and laughs and banter, were curiously compressed.

'Poor Matty!' Lorna said when she returned upstairs. Bob had now given up on the patience and was staring intently at a television commercial, his legs thrust out ahead of him and his hands deep in the pockets of his trousers.

'Why? What's the matter with her now?'

'She seems awfully down. One of her moods.'

'She doesn't take it out on you, does she?'

'No. Of course not!'

'Well, then, why worry?'

'One has to worry about someone for whom one cares. Doesn't one? I mean, that's what it's all about.'

'All what?'

'Friendship. Life.'

'Worrying, like charity, begins at home.'

'Oh, I worry enough about you and Edie!'

'Well, you needn't go on worrying about me. At least not for the moment. I've got a job.'

'A job?' Briefly she imagined that by some miracle he had, in the short while that she had been downstairs in the surgery, somehow, God knows how, found himself a regular job that would take him out of the house the whole of the day and bring in a regular sum each month to his bank account. But he answered:

'Yep. I rang again and there was this thing that had turned up. Shepperton.'

'That means an early start.'

''Fraid so. I can borrow the car, can't I?'

'Oh, Bob, you know how difficult it is for me without it! I mean, if there's some emergency . . . And it's Matty's day off tomorrow, so it's going to be a particularly heavy day.'

Sometimes in the past she had let him have the car and used taxis herself for her house-calls.

He sighed. 'Well, in that case . . . I shall just have to be up at five.'

'No, take it!' she relented. 'Take it! I'll manage somehow.'

'Are you sure?' She knew it to be only a token reluctance.

'Quite sure.'

'It's such hell, that early in the morning. And with this general inefficiency of public transport, one can't even count on arriving on time however early one begins. But can you really survive without it?'

'Yes. I'll hire a car for the afternoon from Mr Appleton. Or take taxis when they're necessary.'

'You'll probably spend more money that way than I'll make.'

She did not contradict what was palpably true.

I I

The next day, while she was lunching off a cheese sandwich and a glass of milk – she only bothered to cook a midday meal if Bob were eating with her – the telephone rang and the nasal voice that she had now learned to recognize as belonging to one of the men who worked at the casting agency said, as always without any other preliminary or any please: 'Robert Ambler.' It was exactly the same tone that Lorna's husband had used when, tired and ailing, he had summoned the next of a long queue of patients into his consulting-room.

'He's out filming, I'm afraid.'

'Filming?' The voice (it always suggested to her someone agile, simian, Jewish) was obviously surprised. 'Are you sure?'

'Yes. He left early this morning – long before I was up. Shepperton, I think.'

There was a pause at the other end of the line. Then: 'Oh, well, thank you.'

'Shall I get him to ring you?'

Hesitation. 'Well . . . Yes – I suppose you could. If he gets back before six. It's a job for tomorrow. Could be three or four days with a bit of luck.' The receiver was replaced at the other end.

Hadn't anyone ever taught him to say please or thank you? That voice had always riled her. But once, when she had said to Bob, 'Next time he uses that tone to me I've a jolly good mind to tell him where to put it,' he had told her, appalled: 'For God's sake, don't do that. Ever. You might ruin all my chances. I need that man. I need him far more than he needs me. He's my bread-and-butter – he and the rest of them. Don't you get it?'

'In that case I wish you could find a more wholesome slice of bread-and-butter.'

'They're in a hurry. That's all it is.'

'I'm in a hurry most of the day. But I don't –'

'Oh, for Christ's sake!'

Six o'clock came and then seven and still Bob had not come home. Minutes past seven he telephoned from a public call-box. 'Don't wait supper for me, Lorna. Endless delays. I've been sitting round on my arse for most of the day, doing damn all in what must be several degrees below freezing-point. It looks as if things are at last starting to move, but God knows when they'll finish.'

'Oh, Bob –' she started, meaning to tell him about the call from the agency. But he cut her short:

'There's my call. See you!'

It was then that she began first to think about the strangeness of that 'Filming? Are you sure?' Spoken in a tone of incredulity. How was it that that agile, simian Jew (yes, she could see him, with his five o'clock shadow and the slight pouches under his dark, melancholy eyes) had not *known* that Bob was out at Shepperton? Well, of course, it was a large organization, that agency, and it might have been someone else who had made the original booking. Bob had often told her that there were hundreds, yes, literally hundreds of people on their files. Far, far too many. That's why work was so scarce, since it had to be rationed among them. But a vague doubt continued to gnaw at one corner of her mind . . .

Long after ten – by then she was starting to prepare for bed – Bob at last came back.

'Christ I'm tired!' he shouted up at her, as she greeted him down the stair-well, her hair loose about her shoulders and her face shiny with cream.

'What kept you so long?'

'Must have something to eat. Famished.' He was hanging up his coat. 'Then a bath. A long, hot bath. You've no idea how cold it was.'

'I'll come down.'

'No, no! I can manage for myself.'

'I've not yet turned in. You make yourself comfortable in the sitting-room – I've left the fire on for you – and I'll bring you a tray.'

'But, Lorna, honestly, I can –'

'Some soup?' she suggested, hurrying down the stairs. 'I've got some lovely home-made tomato soup. I know how you loathe that sweet stuff from a tin, but this is different. And then I can make you an omelette – or some scrambled eggs – or I could even open a tin of –'

'Oh, I leave it to you! I leave it to you! What I need most of all is a stiff drink.'

The skin on his cheekbones, as he looked up at her descending, was the colour and texture of putty. His eyes lacked any lustre. Yes, he's done in, she thought, quite done in. He looks strong, far stronger than myself, but he's not, not really. He'd never survive the sort of life I lead, going out on all those calls in the middle of the night because I can't really expect Matty to take her fair share. 'The evening paper's on the table,' she called as she went into the kitchen.

But when she at last brought the tray in to him, he was not reading the paper. Stretched almost full-length on the sofa, one arm dangling to the floor while the other lay across his eyes, he might have been asleep. 'Here you are! First course!'

'Super!' He roused himself, swinging down his legs and then placing his elbows on his knees as with one hand he rubbed at an inflamed eyelid. 'Just what the doctor ordered.' The last was a shared joke, often repeated, from the time when he was still a schoolboy and she was doing her internship at St Thomas's.

She watched him as he gulped the steaming soup. 'You never had your drink,' she suddenly exclaimed, looking around for his glass.

'Too whacked.'

'I'll fix it for you. What d'you want?'

'The usual.'

The usual was whisky with a splash of soda. She poured it out and then took it across to him:

'Cheers!'

'Cheers!'

'Aren't you going to have a drink to accompany me?'

'Oh, I don't think so.'

'Go on! Be a devil!'

The drink she poured for herself was mostly soda with a dash of whisky. 'I must go and make your omelette.'

'In a moment. No hurry.'

'So it was a pretty beastly day?'

'Beastly. Time-consuming. Pointless. And then they tried to get out of paying us our overtime.'

'Are you on tomorrow?'

'Tomorrow? No, thank God.'

'They didn't get in touch with you at Shepperton?'

'Who?'

'The agency. That man – he rang, you know. Some job.'

'What man? Aronson, you mean?'

'Yes, him. He asked me to ask you to ring him back if you got in before six. I tried to tell you on the telephone but you rang off before I could.'

'Shit! Perhaps he wanted me for that John Huston film.'

'It was odd . . .' Lorna began. Then she stopped, as though her senses had plucked some invisible, inaudible warning out of the air around them.

'What was odd?'

'Well . . .' She hesitated. 'He – he sounded so surprised when I told him you were filming.'

'You told him that?' For a moment he looked not merely taken aback but alarmed, the soup-spoon poised on its way to his lips and those previously lustreless eyes all at once catching fire. 'Why? Why did you have to do that? Why can't you just bloody well leave things alone?' The alarm was turning to anger.

'I couldn't see any harm in it. What on earth does it matter whether I told him or not?'

At that he seemed to make a conscious effort to control himself: 'But, don't you understand, the work I was doing today didn't come to me through them. I didn't want them to know about it. I'm not supposed to get work through any other agencies. That's one of the rules of the game.'

It might have been the voice of Dada, patiently self-restrained, explaining to the youthful Bob why he should have done something that he ought to have done or why he should have done something that he had either forgotten or purposely failed to do. And he was lying, she knew that he was lying! But why? Why?

'I'm sorry,' she said. 'I'm awfully sorry, Bob. I never thought ... It just slipped out. I mean, I naturally assumed ...'

'Sometimes you assume far too much. If I may say so.' That quiet sarcasm was also Dada's.

'I never knew about these other agencies, that was the reason. You've never rung them before, I mean. Have you?'

'I have, as a matter of fact. Once or twice. Not regularly I admit. But on this particular occasion – well, a few days ago I ran into a bloke who runs one of them and it was he who called.'

'Oh. I see.'

'Now do you think you could go and make me that omelette or scrambled eggs or whatever it's going to be?'

'Yes, of course. Sorry.'

She got to her feet. Bob picked up an evening paper and began to open it as she left the room.

As she deftly folded the omelette, remembrance suddenly came to her. *Yep. I rang again and there was this thing that had turned up. Shepperton.* Yes, she was sure that the words were right. And in that case why should he pretend that the work had come through someone else, who had called instead of being called? And why should there have been that initial panic, followed by a rage quite out of proportion to a trivial gaff? Unless, of course, he had never been at Shepperton, had never been filming, had been engaged on something wholly different ... *Oh, Bob, if only you'd talk to me, really talk! I know so little about you, almost nothing.* She had said it so often to him.

'There you are!'

'Marvellous! No one can make an omelette better than you. Do you remember that time you were ill and Matty produced that blackened fritter-thing and then compounded the horror of the deed by scrubbing out your omelette pan? ... Bless you!' He smiled up at her as he took the plate from her, all previous tension gone.

But she had to persist:

'I never knew about this other agency. I thought there was just this one large one –'

'Oh, do we really have to go over all this ground again!'

'I'm only asking out of interest. What concerns you does interest me, you know.'

'There are lots of little agencies. Lots and lots. I'm on the books of the biggest of them but that doesn't mean . . . Oh, do let's drop the subject!'

'What's it called?'

'What's what called?'

'The agency that got you the job today?'

'Let's drop the subject! Lorna, please!' He jumped to his feet. 'I wonder what's on the Third. Isn't it tonight that Solti's doing *Tristan*?'

So they dropped the subject.

12

Matty's mother peered at Lorna's plate – she had recently undergone a cataract operation and the lenses of her glasses now magnified her once beautiful eyes in such a way that they seemed in danger of falling out as she lowered her face closer and closer to it – and asked in that still strong, baritone voice that during the war years had shouted down hecklers at Speakers' Corner: 'Aren't you going to finish that?'

Lorna shook her head, embarrassed. 'Matty's always so generous with her helpings.'

'Well, waste not, want not.' The old woman's hand stretched out and plucked the plate away, with a clinking of the thin band of her wedding-ring against the thick china. 'Eh, Kiki?' She stooped and passed the remains of the fish pie and soggy Brussels sprouts to the obese poodle gazing up at her beseechingly. Lorna almost cried out: 'Be careful! It's full of bones!' but she had not the courage to do so. The dog would have to suffer.

'Well, have some more plonk anyway!' Matty said, splashing Spanish wine from an outsize bottle into Lorna's tumbler.

'Oh, Matty no . . . Please . . .' Ineffectually Lorna attempted to put a hand across the rim. Somehow, when she was invited over by Matty and old Mrs Spencer, she always managed to drink too much, whatever her good resolutions before setting forth. It was as if only by gulping, gulping, gulping at the sweet-sour liquid that she could manage to get down and keep down the food set before her.

Matty's face was flushed. Even a single glass of sherry had that effect on her. 'I'm not offering you any more, Mother, because you shouldn't have had even that first glass.'

'Nonsense.' The old woman half-rose to her feet and grabbed

58

the bottle. Swaying dangerously, she tipped it up and poured until her glass was full to the brim and then beyond it.

'Oh, Mother!' Matty scolded, as she began to mop ineffectually with her paper napkin. 'Why won't you leave that kind of thing to me?'

'I'd be glad to. But when you tell me that I can't have another glass of wine in my own house . . .'

'With your blood-pressure,' Matty muttered.

'Let me do it, Matty,' Lorna volunteered.

But obstinate as ever, Matty refused, levering herself up with one hand and continuing to mop up with the other.

'I hear you're planning a trip?' Lorna shouted at the old woman.

'There's no need to raise your voice dear. With this new aid of mine, I can hear as well as you – probably better.' Mrs Spencer stooped to lift off the floor the plate that the dog had now licked clean and replaced it in front of Lorna once again. Nauseatingly, a single black hair lay diagonally across it. 'Yes, I felt I'd like to see the Hermitage and the Kremlin and, oh, all those wonderful people once again before I die. It's a package tour, of course. That's all I can afford.'

'It's not a question of affording or not affording,' Matty put in crossly, helping herself to some more of the fish pie. 'You can't travel on your own and I've no particular desire to go to that country again.'

'What do you mean – *that country*?'

'You know exactly what I mean.'

For a moment mother and daughter seemed on the verge of one of their long, aimless rounds of bickering. But instead Mrs Spencer turned to Lorna: 'You ought to join us. I know you're not a Party member but I'm sure that somehow we could wangle it.'

'Frankly, I like to go to the sun for my holidays.'

'It's years since you *had* a holiday, a proper holiday of any kind.' Matty removed a bone from between her teeth with a pensive expression. 'You need one,' she announced, in the tone of voice, brooking no contradiction, that she used to tell some nervously undecided patient that she must have a curette.

'Need one? Oh, I don't know.'

'Of course you do. Anyone can see that. You're living on your nerves.'

'That makes it sound as if I'd been disagreeable.'

'Nothing of the kind. If you'd been disagreeable, you might not be in your present state.'

'But I'm not in a state of any kind! I feel perfectly happy. Relaxed. No more overworked than usual.'

'Is that really true?' Matty stared at her, a hand to her forehead, with the stiff grey hair falling over it.

'Do you think we might get on to the next course? If there *is* a next course.' Mrs Spencer's voice was sharp as she massaged Kiki's ears.

'Of course there's a next course. You saw me make a mousse.'

'I'll get it, Matty. Is it in the fridge?' Lorna pushed back her chair; but she knew, even as she spoke, that once again her impulse to go to Matty's aid had been mistaken.

'You'll do no such thing. You entertain Mother, and I'll be back in a jiffy.' Matty was fumbling under her chair for her crutches.

'It's so silly,' Mrs Spencer said as Matty left the room. Her voice was low but Lorna feared that it might not be low enough. 'Why won't she let people do things for her? Pride. That's what it is. Silly pride! I'm still perfectly able, I'm still perfectly strong. But do you think she'll let me raise a finger to help her? You bet your life not! You'd think *I* was the disabled one!'

'I'm afraid it hasn't quite jelled properly.' Matty's mousses rarely did. 'Never mind. It has lashings and lashings of cream in it and four eggs.'

'You're so extravagant in the kitchen,' Mrs Spencer muttered. '*Not* a good manager.'

'Mother – please! *Please!*'

The mousse, slimy and tasting of raw eggs, was almost as difficult to get down as the fish pie before it. Again and yet again Lorna gulped at the rancid wine, until she realized that Mrs Spencer was surveying her with disapproval. She'll be telling everyone I'm turning into an alcoholic, just as she told everyone that that wretched girl opposite was a nymphomaniac merely because she used to watch her from her bedroom window as she kissed her boy-friend good night in the lane at the bottom of the garden.

'A little more?'

Lorna shook her head.

'I'm afraid it's *not* awfully good.'

'Oh, don't go on apologizing for everything, Matty!' Mrs Spencer rose to her feet. 'You'll both excuse me, won't you? I must watch *Mastermind*. I always do. I keep telling Matty not to invite people in on a Thursday evening but of course she never takes a blind bit of notice ... Come along, Kiki! *Kiki!*' Kiki was snuffling in her pelt for fleas.

'She's a wonderful old girl,' Matty said, as the door closed on her mother. Obviously she was glad to be rid of the old woman and to have Lorna to herself at long last.

'Wonderful. I hope I'm like that when I'm in my eighties.'

'Making life hell for everyone else and getting all the fun in the world out of it oneself.'

'You wouldn't want her different. Now would you?'

'Of course not!' Matty struggled again to her feet. 'Let me get the coffee.'

'I'll get it!'

'It's just a question of bringing in the thermos. The cups are out.'

'Well, let me fetch the thermos.'

This time Lorna refused to give way and Matty at last subsided back into her chair with a grunt more of annoyance than of gratitude. The kitchen was in an appalling state, as always, with broken egg-shells lying among dirty pans on the grubby linoleum that was tacked to the surface of the kitchen table, an overflowing dustbin and a sink into which crockery, cutlery and the remains of the meal had all been tipped indiscriminately. Dare I offer to help with the washing-up? But I know what she'll say ...

'Yes, I think you need a holiday,' Matty mused, as she sipped the scalding coffee from the breakfast cup that Lorna had set down before her. Her nose reddened and began to glisten. 'I've been thinking it for quite a time now.'

'I can't imagine why. I feel perfectly fit. I hope I'm efficient. I don't really *enjoy* holidays. I'm a person who must always be doing something. You know that, Matty. You're the same.'

Matty slurped at the cup, lowering her face to it. Then: 'What's on your mind?'

'On my mind?'

'Something's worrying you.'

'Isn't something always worrying everyone? All kinds of things are worrying me – money and that mistake I made in not diagnosing what was wrong with the Robson child sooner and the dreadful state of the garden and, oh, a dozen other trivialities. That's life – a perpetual state of vague worry, or at least, that's what it is for me. "I worry, therefore I am." We all do it – except those of us who are totally brainless or callous.'

'I meant something different.' Again Matty made that ugly slurping noise, like water being sucked down the plug-hole of an old-fashioned bath. 'It's Bob, isn't it?'

'Bob?'

'He's on your mind.' Lorna was silent, stirring her coffee, round and round and round with a hand that hung limply from the wrist. 'Isn't he?'

At last Lorna looked up, her gaze meeting Matty's questing one with a drawn-out reluctance. 'Oh, I worry about him. Yes. Yes, I do.'

'Why?'

'Well . . .' Lorna went on stirring, stirring, stirring.

'Why?' Silence. 'Why, Lorna?'

'Well, I – I worry about what he – he might be doing.' She had not wanted to confess this to Matty or, indeed to anyone else, even to Bob himself. But now that she had done so, the relief was as if, all at once, she had succeeded in voiding the whole revolting meal within her.

'About what he might be doing! If I were you, I should be more worried that he's doing nothing at all. Nothing of any significance, that is.'

Lorna said slowly: 'He's been badly hurt.'

'Badly hurt!' Matty was as contemptuous of the idea as Edie.

'Yes. Badly hurt when he was a boy.' Lorna slowly raised her cup to her lips and let the bitter, lukewarm coffee – God knows how long Matty had boiled the grounds! – settle on her tongue. 'And badly hurt later. When he was abroad.'

'How?'

'How?'

'Yes, how? You go on about something that happened to him in Singapore or Kuala Lumpur or wherever it was. But how do you know that anything happened at all?'

'I know, I just know.' Matty made a scoffing noise at the back of her nose. 'That's the kind of relationship we have – we've always had. He doesn't have to *tell* me things. I just – just know them, that's all.'

'And now this – this sisterly intuition has told you that he's up to something that he oughtn't to be up to?'

Lorna hesitated, her head on one side so that the greying hair fell across a cheek and screened her from the penetrating gaze of her friend and partner. 'At times . . .' she began.

'Yes?'

'Well – at times – I get this – this *dread*. It's irrational of course, totally irrational. I mean he hasn't done anything that would warrant any . . .' (Hasn't he? *Hasn't* he? How about that lie about the filming?) 'And yet – yet . . . Well, I'm worried for him. About him.'

There was a long silence, as Lorna stared down into her empty cup and Matty stared across the table at her. Then Matty said in a curiously vindictive tone:

'You're too close.'

Lorna started, as though her friend had flung the dregs of her coffee in her face. She even put the chilblained fingers of one hand over her mouth and cheek as though to shield herself.

Matty went on: 'Of course, Mother and I are too close, too. It's bad – bad for both of us. But I think your closeness with Bob is even worse.'

Lorna considered for a while; then in a tired, diminished voice she said: 'Well, you may be right. I was a kind of – oh, mother *and* father to him all through those dreadful years. And I suppose that's remained my role ever since. When he took himself off to the Far East, perhaps it was a deliberate effort to – to emancipate himself. But . . . it failed.'

'Perhaps you wanted it to fail.' Again Lorna started, with that gesture of fingers over mouth and cheek, as the words, soft and insidious now, came across the table at her. 'Secretly. Subconsciously.'

'I don't know,' Lorna answered at last. 'Perhaps I did. I was becoming very lonely – with Alfred gone and Edie getting restless and unresponsive. I'm not *good* at loneliness.'

'Unlike me. I'm a marvel at it.' Suddenly Matty had changed again; her voice was loud and jolly. 'More coffee?'

Lorna shook her head. 'I won't sleep.'

'I can always sleep. That's the one great consolation I've always had in life. Nothing can keep me from sleeping. Ever.'

'Well, I envy you that.'

The door creaked open and Kiki pattered in, followed by Mrs Spencer.

'Would you believe it! That idiotic woman – her speciality, her *speciality*, mind you, is supposed to be English literature – was under the impression that Mr Knightley was a character in *Pride and Prejudice*. Well, after that, I just gave up. I couldn't be bothered any longer.'

'You ought to enter yourself.'

Matty's irony was lost on her mother.

'Oh, I've better things to do with my time, thank you, Matty dear!'

13

'I hope this doesn't mean she's never going to come to us again.' Lorna was speaking of Mrs Emerson, who had given the two consulting-rooms and the waiting-room a perfunctory going-over but who had again said that she was too busy with her grandchildren to clean upstairs that day.

'Why should it mean that? Those brats aren't a permanent fixture, are they? I thought she was looking after them only for the five days that that daughter of hers was on a spree in Tangiers.'

'I have a hunch. I don't know.'

'What kind of hunch?'

'I think she's offended.'

'With us?'

Lorna nodded, transfixing another crumpet with the toasting-fork.

'But why? Why?'

It astonished her that he should have to ask that. She held the fork out towards the gas fire that had already made her cheeks rosy and shiny. 'Well, you did rather go for her yesterday.'

An inveterate breaker, Mrs Emerson had dropped the Buddhist relic, a tortoise supporting on its back a miniature glass pagoda containing some transparent pebbles that were said to be the calcined bones of a Buddha, that stood in the centre of the mantelpiece of Bob's room, with photographs of Lorna and their dead mother on either side of it and a dusty accumulation of picture postcards, often three and four thick, propped up behind. The china of the tortoise's shell had been smashed into fragments on the tile surround of the gas fire and the pebbles, like so many tiny, asymmetrical lumps of resin, had been scattered in all directions: under the bed, under the fire, into the pile of the carpet. At first Mrs Emerson had been unaware of the enormity of her crime, announcing with no obvious contrition or dismay: 'I'm terribly sorry, Mr Ambler, but I seem to have had an accident with that tortoise thing of yours.'

Bob had jumped to his feet, throwing down the evening paper. 'You've *what*?'

'One moment it was in my hand and the next moment it wasn't.'

'Have you any idea of how valuable that *tortoise thing* is – or, rather, was?'

Mrs Emerson's face suddenly set into lines of injured obduracy. 'I don't know anything about that.'

'That *tortoise thing*, as you like to call it, was a *shari*. I hardly expect you to know what a *shari* is. But it contained, for your information, some extremely important Buddhist relics.'

'I've swept up all the pieces. They're all on your table by the window.'

'Kindly leave them alone!' Bob was now shouting at her. 'Don't touch them! Don't go back into that room! You've done enough harm already!'

As Mrs Emerson began to back away from him towards the door, Lorna intervened in a nervous attempt to placate her: 'You could do out the dining-room, Mrs Emerson. How about that?'

Mrs Emerson did not answer. She left the room and a moment later Lorna heard her open the hall cupboard in which she always hung her coat. 'That bloody woman! That bloody, bloody woman!' Bob was muttering. Lorna went out.

'Are you going, Mrs Emerson?'

'Yes, I'm going, Dr Martin. I think it would be better. Anyone can break something. Accidents do happen.' She was breathless as she spoke to Lorna, her eyes averted as she struggled to get first one arm and then the other into the new coat that had been a birthday present from her daughter and son-in-law. 'We've all had accidents at some time or other.' She was now making her way towards the door. 'You broke that vase only last week,' she said, wrenching at the latch. 'And he dropped that casserole. I suppose he's forgotten that.' Wind whirled through the open door; then it slammed.

Lorna turned and found her brother close behind her.

'How *could* she?'

Then he moved away and began to mount the stairs.

Lorna followed him.

He stood by the table, staring in consternation at the two little piles made by Mrs Emerson: one of pebbles and one of shards of china. Slowly he picked up one of the pebbles and trickled it back and forth in his palm.

'I could probably stick it together for you. I have that special German glue. It's marvellous stuff.'

'Oh, don't be such an idiot! For Christ's sake!'

'It won't be the same, of course. But I'm sure I could –'

'It's such – such bad luck.'

The single glistening, semi-transparent pebble still trickled up and down his palm; and, suddenly stricken, Lorna realized that he was, yes, frightened – that was the only word for it.

'You know, I had terrible difficulty in getting the dealer to sell it. He was a Japanese in Singapore – I often bought things from him. But this – this he didn't want me to have. To a Buddhist it's what a fragment of the True Cross is to a Catholic. No Catholic would want a pagan to get his hands on such an object. And now this stupid bitch . . .'

'Let me try to mend it for you. Please!' Suddenly noticing that there was a little pebble gleaming up from the pile of the carpet beside his left foot, she began to stoop for it.

'Oh, leave it!' he shouted at her as he had shouted at Mrs Emerson. But she picked up the pebble between finger and thumb and carefully added it to the little heap.

Bob pulled open the drawer of his desk and snatched a manila envelope. 'What are you doing?' Without answering, he began to pick up the fragments of china and dropped them inside. Then he scooped up the pebbles.

'But I could mend it for you.'

Still saying nothing, he placed the envelope back in another drawer, already full of cigarette cards that he had once collected as a schoolboy.

'Please! Oh, please let me try!'

'Forget it.'

'But Bob, I know that I could –'

'Forget it!'

. . . And perhaps he had, indeed, forgotten the envelope containing the shards of china and those strange bead-like pebbles. But Lorna could not forget either them or that panic and rage of his when he had first examined them lying on the table; and she was sure that Mrs Emerson had not forgotten either.

'Well, I was bloody annoyed,' he now said. 'The way she came out with it! It might have been a saucer or teacup.'

'You can hardly expect a woman like that to know the value of a *shari*. Be reasonable! To her it's just an ornament – like those awful china scotties that Matty has on her mantelpiece downstairs.'

'It makes me sick – physically sick – to think about it. It was old, terribly old. And it – it had this tremendous religious significance. Breaking it like that could bring us terrible luck. And . . . Oh, it's pointless to try to explain to you. I might as well try to explain to Mrs Emerson.'

'Thank you,' Lorna retorted bitingly.

14

After he had gone out that evening – 'I have this bloke I have to
see, I'll be back for supper' and the door had slammed behind
him – Lorna fetched the ancient, ramshackle vacuum-cleaner and
a duster from the cupboard under the staircase and began to
do out her room. She hated housework and, grateful for Mrs
Emerson's perfunctory visits, preferred not to notice the dust that
collected against the skirting-boards, filmed the telephones and
lay thick along the tops of the picture-frames. It was only in the
kitchen that she insisted on absolute cleanliness, often going down
on her knees to scrub the floor herself after Mrs Emerson had
pushed a damp, sour-smelling mop back and forth across it before
rushing off.

How on earth could I have failed to *see* how filthy this room has
become over the last few months? She suppressed a shudder as
she dragged her bed away from the wall and saw the fat rolls of
fluff lurking beneath it. Perhaps Bob had, after all, been right to
shout at Mrs Emerson. She rarely put in more than and hour and
a half of the two hours due from her and much of that time was
spent in drinking what she called 'Nes'. At first angrily and then
with increasing pleasure, Lorna set about a thorough spring-
clean: taking down the pictures, stacking the chairs on top of each
other in a corner, brushing the dust away from the skirting-boards
on her hands and knees. The sweat began to trickle off her nose
and chin and to run between her breasts; her hair grew lank.

Next it was the turn of Bob's room. His was the same high brass
bedstead in which Dada used to sleep after he and their mother
had ceased to share a room – the room now occupied by Lorna.
Lorna had wanted to get rid of it, but, astonishingly, since she
had not imagined that Bob would wish to sleep in a bed once
occupied by someone he had so much hated, he had said, 'Oh, no,

I like it. It's the kind of bed I like. And besides, brass beds are now very much in.' The whole room had hardly changed since Dada's time, except that there was no longer that smell of expensive lavender water masking another faintly insidious smell, as of the lair of some wild animal, long vacated. There were still the two Stubbs prints, 'Haymaking' and 'Ploughing', facing each other; still that circular mirror, blotched and cracked across one corner, on its mahogany Victorian stand surfaced with a marble that looked like a slice of raw beef oozing blood; still the stud-box of Florentine leather with Dada's initials elaborately entwined on it. Dada's silver-backed brushes, even the yellowing ivory of Dada's comb. How could Bob bear to have all these reminders of Dada round him? Or did he get a pleasure out of running that comb through his hair as he peered into that mirror, Dada's mirror, and told himself: 'Well, you bastard, I survived you! I've had the last word!'

Under the bed – it squealed as Lorna pulled it out into the centre of the room – Bob had piled, in a higgledy-piggledy jumble, a number of battered suitcases, pairs and pairs of dusty shoes, a trunk, innumerable cardboard boxes, most of them containing old magazines about cars or sailing or horses, and, its edges bound in brass, the old wooden tuck-box that she remembered from his schooldays. Lorna sneezed and sneezed again as she began to dust off one object after another. She'd really have to ask Bob, at the risk of being told to mind her own business, if he wanted to keep all these shoes, many of them in need of repair and most of them no longer worn. The majority of the suitcases were empty and she began to put one inside another, like a series of Chinese boxes. Others contained tropical suits fading at the edges; bow-ties dating from his university years; letters from herself, from Mother, even from Alfred, but never, oh never, from Dada; photographs of people he had known at school – yes, that was the boy who had died of leukaemia, only seventeen – or at Cambridge or out in the Far East. Forgetting that it had been her original purpose to clean out the room, she turned them over, fascinated, as though somewhere among them she would find a clue, perhaps the one essential clue to – well, what?

She roused herself, looking at her watch. It had gone seven and Bob would soon be back for the supper that they usually ate at eight. This suitcase would just fit into the tuck-box. But when she attempted to open the tuck-box, she found that it was locked. Certainly it contained something – she had realized that when she had first moved it – but what it contained was nothing of any weight. She pulled the box towards her, leaning back on her heels as she knelt on the floor beside the bed. She tipped it up. Something slid with a rustle and a dull thud within it. What? She felt suddenly anxious, unhappy, exasperated, and could not think why. Then she remembered . . .

'It's locked!'

'Leave it alone!'

She was seated on the tuck-box, under the window of the attic room that he occupied next to hers, and idly, with no purpose, the fingers of one hand had picked at the hasp.

'Why do you keep it locked? What's in it? Tell me.'

She was eighteen at the time and he was eleven.

'Nothing.'

'Then why keep it locked?'

'Why shouldn't I keep it locked? It's my box, isn't it? I can do what I like with it, can't I?'

'Yes, of course.' She had laughed and then, hardly realizing what she was doing, she had got off the box and raised it by one of the handles. Something within it – perhaps a number of things – had shifted downwards. She had heard two sounds, first a slither and then a dull thud.

'But it's *not* empty!'

He had got off his bed and come slowly towards her, with a chilling mixture of panic and fury not unlike his panic and fury when he had first inspected the fragments of the *shari*.

'I told you not to touch it. Leave it alone! It's none of your business!'

'All right, all right!' And she had again laughed, though she had not felt like laughing. 'If you want your little secrets, then have your little secrets.'

A few days later Dada had taken him to the Science Museum –

71

it was a period when the stepfather was still forcing himself to attempt to treat the boy as a son – and their mother was busy with one of the innumerable committees on which she had begun to sit as soon as the years of chronic invalidism were behind her and forgotten. Lorna had gone from her own attic room into the one next to it. At the time it had seemed merely an impulse, engendered by the boredom of the medical textbook on which she had been working and her isolation in the cold, ugly house. But later she had come to admit to herself that all along she had planned to do just this.

The tuck-box had vanished. It was no longer under the window and she could not find it under the bed or in the massive wardrobe. But inset high up on one of the sloping walls of the room there was a little trapdoor that led to a loft. From this loft came an incessant sound of dripping day and night, punctuated by a rapid drumming or a rushing noise whenever anyone in any part of the house turned on a tap. Lorna, guided by some obscure instinct, now tugged at this door until, reluctantly, almost as though it too were locked like the tuck-box, it came away. She stood on tiptoe and peered. Something glimmered at her.

Yes, it was the box. She fetched a torch and then, unable to pull herself up into the loft despite repeated attempts to do so, she fetched the steps from the kitchen. As she was mounting the steps, she thought: I can't break open the lock. I'll have to try some other way. And then she went back into her own attic room and brought her keys.

It was far easier than she had ever imagined. The third key, the key to one of her own three suitcases, turned effortlessly and her fingers raised first the hasp and then the dusty lid. She shone the torch downwards, wishing that the battery were stronger. It caught – yes! – that hair-ribbon she had lost, oh, months and months ago. And – could it be? – that suspender-belt that had so mysteriously vanished while she was away for a weekend (she and her mother had both suspected the Mrs Emerson of that time) . . . And an amber bracelet (she had never even realized that it was missing, she had forgotten all about it until this moment) . . . And, strangest of all, a sanitary-towel packet, unopened . . .

She stared in turn at each of these objects, hardly daring to touch them, as though each were something both soiled and soiling. She felt sickened and yet exhilarated – rather as she had felt after she and Bob had gone together on the helter-skelter at the Clapham Common fair on his eleventh birthday a few days before. What did it all *mean*? Why on earth should he have wanted to steal – yes, there was no other word for it – this extraordinary accumulation of objects from her?

She closed the lid slowly, thoughtfully; and then she put down the hasp and inserted the key. Having moved so effortlessly before in the lock, this time it grated and jarred as she forced it round. Her finger-marks were in the dust of the lid. But she did not care about that.

She jumped down from the loft ignoring the steps, and all at once that dripping, dripping, dripping of the cistern, of which she had been totally unaware while standing only a few feet away from it, now began to throb in her head and down her spine and then to hammer at the small of her back with louder and louder and sharper and sharper persistence. She sank on to his bed and stared at her hands, which were grey with dust and trembled slightly as they grasped the torch between them.

What did it all *mean*?

She never asked him, either then or later. She would never ask him now or in the future. She had suddenly jumped off his bed and run, yes, literally run out of the room as though that ceaseless, steady drip-drip-drip above her and behind her were the ticking of some bomb.

15

'God, what tosh!' The queue moved slowly towards the single harassed woman behind the cloakroom counter.

'Do you really think so?' Fascinated, Lorna had been watching the attendant as she snatched the tickets and then hunted feverishly along the racks. Though in such a hurry, she never failed to glance over to assess the size of any tip that was dropped into her saucer.

'Of course. High-class tosh, but tosh none the less.'

An elderly woman, with a fillet of jet beads around dishevelled grey locks and more jet beads, ropes and ropes of them, dangling from her neck, swung round and gave them each in turn a disdainful up-and-down stare. Then she swung away again and said something inaudible to her equally elderly male companion and they both gave identical braying laughs, except that one was an octave above the other.

'Bob!' What Lorna first saw was the freckled hand, with its beautifully manicured, square nails, clamped on her brother's shoulder. 'What a lucky chance! Now you'll be able to save me some queuing.' Was that accent vaguely Australian? And where had she heard it previously?

'Harry,' Bob said, and swallowed. 'Harry. Fancy seeing you here.' He seemed visibly to have shrunk under the weight of the hand.

'I'm not totally uncultured.' The man held out his two cloak-room tickets and a tenpenny piece. 'Here. You do have a wonderful knack of turning up when one's most in need of help.'

By now Lorna had raised her eyes from the hand on her brother's shoulder. She saw a powerfully heavy torso, surmounted by a thin, wrinkled neck – not at all the kind of neck that she would have expected, the neck of an old man or of an invalid – and a narrow head in which the mouth and the eyes looked like horizontal incisions under reddish hair cut unfashionably close *en brosse*. This man was far taller than anyone else around them and, unlike almost anyone else, he was wearing a dinner-jacket with a bootlace bow-tie and an elaborately frilled shirt. Cold blue eyes now gazed at her out of their slits.

'This is my sister, Lorna.'

'Hello, Lorna.'

'Hello,' she responded, riled by the familiarity of the Christian name. She had not intended to shake hands with him, but, when he put out his own, she reluctantly went out to meet it.

'This is Harry Van Fleet.'

'My wife. Avril.'

Lorna had not noticed the woman before. Avril, April ... Yes, in that shimmering dress of pale green taffeta, with a cloud of ash-blonde hair fluffed around the pallor of a small, beaky face, she was like some tremulous, showery day of early spring. This time it was Lorna who put her hand out first, and the other woman who reluctantly took it in icy fingers after a second of hesitation.

'What a play, what a terrific play!' Van Fleet exclaimed, the four of them now bunched up together in the slow-moving queue.

'She was marvellous, wasn't she?' Bob said, not contradicting a verdict that Lorna knew to be totally at variance with his own.

'Oh, marvellous, marvellous!' Yes, Lorna decided, those vowels could only be Australian.

The wife gave her head a little shake, so that the hair like spun-sugar swayed from side to side. The movement might possibly have been intended as a mute indication of dissent.

'You've never even told me about your sister. Why have you always kept her a secret from me?'

'Of course I've mentioned her to you. Often.' Bob was embarrassed, staring down at the cloakroom tickets that he held between the forefingers and thumbs of both his hands, his and Lorna's in his left hand and the Van Fleets' in his right. Lorna knew that he was lying; and she also knew that this encounter was something that he would never have wished to happen.

'Your brother likes to play his cards very close to his chest.

Which is not always a fault, of course.' Van Fleet's large, freckled left hand went to the bootlace tie and caressed one end of it.

Bob had reached the counter.

'There you are, Mrs Van Fleet. That's yours, I think.' So she was not Avril to him, though her husband was Harry; and the respectful formality with which he helped her into the lavender-grey coat lined with – could it be? – mink, confirmed that he hardly knew her.

'Thank you.' She blinked her pale eyelashes nervously as she began to do up the buttons.

'Lorna!' He gave her coat a rough upward jerk so that the sleeves caught her sharply at the armpits. Oh God, of course, a button would have to be dangling by what appeared to be a single thread!

Harry Van Fleet's coat had a sumptuous astrakhan collar, which made that curiously scrawny neck look even scrawnier. The four of them drifted towards the doors and then out into the street.

'Where's that bloody man?' the Australian muttered.

His wife pointed: 'There.' She waved an arm and, as she did so, a huge Mercedes began to glide towards them.

'You've got transport, I suppose?'

'As a matter of fact, Lorna's car has packed it in. We should have had it back this afternoon but of course . . . Anyway, it's only a step to Leicester Square station.'

'Good grief, man, we can easily give you both a lift. Where is it you have to go?'

'Parson's Green. But there's honestly no need . . .' Lorna knew that this was no formal reluctance to accept the offer; it was real. 'The station's just around the corner . . .'

'But Parson's Green is actually on our way. Isn't it, Smiley?'

The moustached chauffeur – an ex-guardsman, Lorna would have guessed – replied: 'Well, almost, sir. Almost.' He was holding the back door open.

'As near as makes no difference. Hop in, Lorna!' Van Fleet's hand closed on her arm, just above the elbow, and propelled her forward. Lorna got in. 'I'll sit in front. You get in the back with the two ladies, Bob.'

Lorna felt the softness of the mink-lined coat against her leg.

Although it was like the gentlest of caresses, she at once withdrew from it.

Bob said, his voice unusually high: 'What a super car!'

'You've seen it before,' Harry turned round to answer.

'Oh, yes, of course. But it *is* a super car. Isn't it, Lorna?'

Lorna nodded.

'Yes, we can easily pass through Parson's Green on our way to Chiswick. No difficulty at all. After all, you rescued us over our coats. But for you, we might still be standing in that queue.'

A long silence followed, with the three occupants of the back seat all staring straight ahead of them. Then Harry asked:

'Do you and Bob live together, Lorna?' He did not turn round on this occasion.

'Yes, that's right.' She still felt irritated each time that he addressed her by her Christian name.

'Temporarily,' Bob said, to Lorna's amazement. 'Until I find a place of my own. You know what it's like in London today. Prices are astronomical. And Lorna has this huge, rather hideous Victorian house – her surgery's in it too – and so –'

'Surgery?'

'I'm a doctor.'

'Now why on earth didn't you ever tell me that you had a sister who was a doctor?'

'But I did, I did.'

'No, Bob. No.' Van Fleet chuckled, turning away from them. 'You *are* an odd one, I must say, and no mistake. I never even knew – never guessed – that you didn't live alone.'

'The trouble is that you never listen.'

'The trouble is that you never talk.'

Van Fleet began to ask Lorna about her work. 'I suppose most of your patients are NHS,' he said, as though that were something discreditable, and she answered tersely:

'I have no private patients.'

'But you'd make an exception for me, wouldn't you?' He intended it to be playful but somehow he failed.

'Oh, of course!' Bob put in when Lorna did not answer. 'That goes without saying.'

'The only problem is that I'm so disgustingly healthy! Never a day of illness in my life. It's Avril who's always got something or other wrong with her.'

In silence, Mrs Van Fleet continued to stare straight out ahead of her at the back of the chauffeur's close-cropped, raw-looking neck.

Soon Bob was saying: 'You can let us out here.'

'You don't live above that garage, do you?'

'No. But you don't want all the bother of turning off.'

'No bother at all. Just tell Smiley where he should turn.'

Lorna knew that Bob did not wish this man to know precisely where they lived. But if Van Fleet set his mind to it, he would have no difficulty in discovering the address; and, besides, what possible reason could there be for concealment? Snobbery might have accounted for a reluctance to confess to living in Parson's Green – whatever the Thurstons might have condescendingly said the other evening about the whole neighbourhood having 'gone up'; but the house, though architecturally a disaster, was in fact imposing by the standards of that area.

'Well, it's the third turning on the right,' Bob said, raising a gloved hand to his mouth and giving a little nervous cough behind it. How well Lorna knew that cough, first developed under Dada's sardonic onslaughts. 'Yes, here. That's it.'

Silently the chauffeur managed to convey both exasperation and contempt as he swung the wheel round; and the contempt still remained as he jumped out to open the door for them.

Since Bob was evidently not going to make the offer, Lorna felt compelled to say out of politeness: 'Would you like to come in for a nightcap?'

Though the invitation was addressed, not to Van Fleet but to his wife, it was Van Feet who answered: 'Awfully good of you. But Avril gets anxious about the kids. It's silly of her but she doesn't really trust our new *au pair* and Smiley's wife's away on a visit to a sick aunt.'

'Sister,' Smiley corrected.

'Well, then . . .' The razor-sharp wind was scraping at Lorna's bare legs as she stooped to the window. 'Thank you. Thank you very much.'

'Not at all. Always delighted to oblige.'

As the limousine glided off down the dark, slithery road, Lorna suddenly thought: She never said a word, not a single word, throughout the journey. Not even goodbye.

Bob was fumbling for his latch-key.

'Who is he?'

'Who?'

'Harry Van Fleet.'

'Christ, how this stove is stinking again! Shouldn't it be cleaned?'

'I'll tell Mrs E. Unless you felt like cleaning it yourself.'

'Oh, I suppose I could do that,' he said, slipping his coat from his shoulders.

'You did say a long time ago . . .'

'Yes, I know, I know. Now don't nag. Please!'

'It was you who first mentioned the subject of the stove.'

'Now don't *nag*!'

'Tell me about him.'

Bob was silent, as he wandered into the sitting-room; he might not have heard her, though obviously he had.

'Bob!'

'I hardly know him.'

'How did you meet him?'

'How does one meet people? I honestly don't remember.'

'Have you known him long?'

'Oh I suppose I've seen him off and on for two or three years. He's one of those friends of friends. I really know him awfully little. And I know awfully little about him.'

'He's an Australian, isn't he?'

'Yes, I suppose he is.'

'But she's not?'

He was punching the buttons of the television set, so that a glimpse of one programme was followed instantaneously by a glimpse of another and then another.

'Must you do that, Bob?'

He switched off the set.

'She's not?'

'No. I think I heard somewhere – from someone or other – that she came of this family of merchant bankers. But I may have got it wrong.'

'What does he do?' Silence. 'Bob, what does he *do*?'

'Oh, I honestly can't remember ... Yes, property, I think. A developer.'

'And I imagine that it was *her* money that gave him his start?'

'Could be. Something like that. Anyway he's got pots and pots of his own money now. You could see that – his coat, her coat, the car, that snooty driver of theirs. Not in my league at all, as I told you.' He was looking down at his hands, holding them out before him as though inspecting them for stains or cuts. 'How about some grub?' he asked. 'I'm absolutely famished.'

'I'll go and put it out.' Before leaving, she had prepared a hurried supper of *quiche*, salad and baked apples.

'I must have a wash.' He was still staring at his hands.

Over the meal, Lorna said: 'That voice of his. It was exactly like that voice on the telephone.'

'What voice?'

'That man I spoke to the other day. Don't you remember?'

He shook his head.

'You must remember. He was furious because you'd made an appointment for the evening and then let him down.'

'That man wasn't Harry!'

'Wasn't it?'

'Of course not. That was someone totally different. Someone – an old bore – that I met in K.L. I told you that.'

'Anyway, there's something about this Van Fleet man that I don't like at all.'

'He's all right. He's done me a good turn from time to time.'

She pondered for a moment and then said: 'You know, I found him ... vaguely sinister.'

'Sinister! There's nothing *sinister* about him. You do get the most extraordinary ideas ... I agree that he's tough, he's ruthless, he's not the most sensitive man in the world – in spite of his taste

80

for Pinter and his collection of Impressionists and his shelves and shelves of records. But sinister . . .'

There was a long silence. Then Lorna ventured:

'And I'd guess she was unhappy.'

'Could be. I've no idea.'

'I felt it. In the car. The way she said nothing, not a word. And, even more, the way she hardly moved. Just staring straight ahead at the back of that chauffeur's neck.'

'I expect she's shy. Some people are, you know. Not everyone has your self-confidence.' Suddenly his voice had a sarcastic edge to it.

'I don't think I'd care to be married to a man like that. I don't think I'd like it at all.'

Bob got to his feet, though the plate before him was still half-full. He crossed over to the sink. 'Well, you're not married to him. So why worry?'

'What are you doing? Don't you want to eat any more?'

He turned the tap and then, wrists nerveless, held first one hand and then the other beneath it. There was a remote, absorbed expression on his face, as though he were lost in some private dream.

'What are you doing?' she repeated.

'I just remembered. I forgot to wash my hands.'

'But, Bob, you . . .'

She broke off; something warned her that it was better not to say it. While taking the food out of the refrigerator, she had heard the ancient plumbing gurgling and thudding. It was not for the first time that he was now washing his hands.

16

Some two weeks after that encounter at the theatre, Lorna break-fasted alone. She had been out to dinner with the Thurstons, but Bob, though also invited, had said that it would be a good opportunity to pop over to see some friends. 'What friends?' she had inevitably asked; and no less inevitably he had replied: 'Oh, friends, that's all. You've never met them. An American couple over here on a visit,' he had added, sensing her dissatisfaction.

She had not heard him come home – it must have been extremely late because she herself had not put out her light until long after one – and when she had taken him his usual early-morning cup of tea, he had groaned, shielded his eyes from the light that came through the open door, one hand laid across them, and had muttered, 'Oh, let me sleep, let me sleep!' So she had put the cup down on the bedside table and had then left him to it. By his bed (she saw them again now as she bit ruminatively into a slice of bread scorched in the erratic toaster that Bob was still always promising to fix) his shoes had been abandoned, one flung horizon-tally across the other. Both were caked with mud. Where could he have taken his American friends to get them in that state? He had borrowed the car – she had herself taken the underground to the Thurstons – but he could hardly have set off for the country in it late on a winter's evening.

'Blast!' She said it aloud, as once again she saw the acrid black smoke rising from the toaster. Then, at the precise moment when she was jerking up the charred slices of toast – this time they would be totally inedible – the telephone began to ring. Lorna had a friend, an insomniac with a hyperthyroid condition, who thought nothing of ringing up at half past seven, seven or even half past six, often prefacing the conversation with a cheerful, 'I know this is terribly early to ring but I simply had to tell you . . .' No doubt it was she.

'Hello!'

'Could I speak to Bob Ambler, please?'

She knew that voice at once: this time there was no mistaking it. But Van Fleet was evidently in no mood to waste time on a greeting to her.

'I'm afraid he's still asleep.'

'Asleep!'

'Yes. He had a late night. He asked me not to wake him. Can I give him a message for you?'

There was a pause; then in an almost exact repetition of their previous telephone conversation, Van Fleet replied in a tone of barely controlled rage: 'Yes. Tell him Harry Van Fleet called. Ask him what the hell happened to him last night. Ask him why he never showed up. Tell him I don't like to have my time wasted. Tell him I waited the whole evening.'

'Is that all?' She felt the receiver trembling in her hand.

'Tell him to call me. At my office. Just as soon as he comes out of that beauty sleep of his. Harry Van Fleet.'

'Yes, I know who it is.'

But, as before, the telephone had clicked and died on her before she had succeeded in getting the whole of her last sentence out.

Slowly she cut two more slices of bread to replace the wasted ones. This time, too, Van Fleet had spoken of Bob as an employer might speak of one humble employee to another humble employee – as he might speak of Smiley if the chauffeur had failed to bring round the Mercedes at the precise hour specified. What right had he to give orders to Bob, much less to herself, in such an insulting tone? She told herself that he was just another brash, rich, ambitious Australian, used to imposing his will on people weaker or politer than himself; but somehow that explanation was not adequate.

As she went on eating, she scribbled a note with a hand that still shook with anger: 'Harry Van F. telephoned. Asked why you hadn't turned up last night. Said would you phone – at office. Sounded pretty shirty. L.' And all the time she was thinking:

83

There's something between them – something of which I know nothing, which Bob is keeping secret. But what? What? She folded the note in two and left it in the toast-rack, so that he could not fail to see it.

'Are you off?'

She was opening the door that led to the basement stairs when there he was above her, one hand sleepily kneading at an eye. His colour was ghastly. If she did not know that, because of his diabetes, he never drank to excess, she would have concluded that he was suffering from a paralysing hangover. 'Who the hell was that ringing just now? The bell woke me.'

'Your pal.'

'Which pal?'

'The pal you were supposed to be meeting last evening. Apparently you forgot.'

'Harry?'

'Yes. Harry. He didn't sound too pleased.'

'Shit!' He was now hurrying down the stairs, tightening the sash of his paisley-silk dressing-gown with nervous, plucking gestures.

'I thought him bloody rude. He didn't even bother to speak to me by name but he must have known who I was. I might have been a skivvy from his tone.'

'What did he say?'

'Well, I've told you. He wants you to ring him back. Just as soon, he said, as you'd woken from your beauty sleep. So that's what you'd better do.' Her sense of exclusion from this mysterious relationship between the two men made her tone hard, even bitchy. 'At his office. I presume you know the number? He didn't volunteer it.'

'Yes, I know the number.' Still the nervous plucking gestures at the sash. 'But Christ, I wish he wouldn't –' He broke off.

'Did you have a date with him?' Hearing the voices of Matty and Mrs Emerson coming up from the basement, she shut the door again.

Bob hesitated. 'Not really. I *half* said . . . Nothing definite.'

'Well, he certainly sounded as if he had thought that it was definite. What had you planned to do?'

'Planned to do? What do you mean?'

'Well, were you going to the theatre together or the cinema or a pub or what?'

'Oh, I was just going over for a drink and a chat. That's all. Nothing else. I don't know why he should have ...' Again he broke off.

'Well, I'm late, I'd better be off.' She pulled the door open again. She wished that she could stay to hear what he had to say to Van Fleet. 'You'd better make yourself some fresh tea. And I'm afraid we're out of bacon.'

'Oh, I couldn't face bacon. In fact I don't think I can face anything but a pot of tea.'

'You must have made a night of it.'

'What?'

She heard the monosyllable but did not answer as she closed the intervening door behind her and clattered down the stairs.

Matty, seated at the desk in her consulting-room, looked up with hooded eyes through her half-open door, as Lorna hurried past.

'Hello, love.'

'Oh, hello, Matty. How are things?'

'Could be worse ... I must say you've got that car of yours into a nice mess. Where've you been in it?'

'The car ...? Oh, Bob was out in it last night.'

'I might have known! Looks as if it had been driven across a ploughed field. You'd better try to get him to clean it for you.'

'Yes, he was visiting some friends in the country,' Lorna lied. She had to restrain herself from hurrying up the area steps to inspect the car there and then.

'He ought to buy himself a car of his own. You're far too longsuffering. And you know – and I know – that it's going to be you that eventually takes the car to the car-wash.'

'Oh, Matty, please!'

'It's odd that the people who have all the time in the world have the least time to spare.'

Lorna walked on to her own consulting-room. Then, having given it a brief inspection, she called out: 'Oh, Mrs Emerson! *Mrs Emerson!*'

'Yes?'

A scarf tied about her head and a brush in one hand, Mrs Emerson first peered round the door of the waiting-room, where she had been chatting to the solitary patient already seated there, and then reluctantly approached.

'Have you done out this room?'

'Yes, of course.' Mrs Emerson was obviously offended by the question.

'Then all I can say is that you've not done it out very well,' Lorna retorted with that same uncharacteristic hardness, even bitchiness of tone that she had already used to Bob. 'This waste-paper basket hasn't been emptied. And the wash-basin . . .'

'I've done my best in the time available.'

'Well, your best has not been good enough.'

Lorna shut the door with an angry push. But a moment later Matty had opened it and come in, closing it again behind her.

'We don't want to lose her,' she warned.

'She's so bloody inefficient. At least she used once to clean this part of the house thoroughly but now it's even worse than upstairs.'

'Nonsense. She's cleaning no better and no worse than she's ever done. She's always forgetting the waste-paper baskets and the wash-basins. You know that as well as I do. She's not perfect – far from it – but, as she often says herself, which of us is perfect? We'll be lucky to find anyone else as good.'

'All right, Matty! All right!'

Lorna covered her eyes with a hand, flinching, as though the light from the electric bulb above her were too dazzling.

'Lorna . . .' Matty swayed perilously across the room. 'What's the matter? What is it?'

'Nothing. Nothing at all. I just can't stand all this – this *mess* and inefficiency . . .'

'There'll always be mess and inefficiency in this country. More and more of it. So you'd better reconcile yourself.' Almost toppling as she stood above Lorna, Matty put a hand on her shoulder. There were callouses in the cleft between thumb and forefinger and the hand itself had grown extremely strong from that perpetual levering and grasping.

'Matty, I must get started.' Lorna pressed the button that lit up a sign in the waiting-room to summon her patients. She would have preferred to go and call the patients personally when she was ready for them as in the time of Dada and Alfred, but this new system was obviously better for Matty. 'You know how Monday is always our busiest day.'

Matty sighed. 'All right, pet. I'll leave you to it.' She turned and all but collided with Mrs Page, who had come for a renewal of her prescription for her 'happiness pills'.

17

Miranda Thurston arrived at the restaurant with two carrier bags from Harrods. 'Be a poppet, Luigi, and store those somewhere for me . . . Darling, I'm afraid I'm terribly, terribly late. Do forgive me. But shopping is *hell* at this time of year. I was feeling anything but good will to all men – or all women, for that matter – as I struggled from counter to counter.'

'I'll have to be quick. I've got two afternoon calls.'

'But I thought that Thursday was the day when that cripple woman – Mitty or Matty or whatever it is – took charge! I wanted you to come on to the Chinese exhibition with me. I've been twice already but there's far too much to digest at one visit or even two. Oh, Lorna! Honestly!'

'Everyone's ill at this time of year. Matty just can't cope on her own – any more than I can.'

'It's too bad! Well, never mind, we must make the most of the little time we have together . . . Thank you, Luigi.' She took the menu from the head waiter and stared shortsightedly at it. Evidently she was not wearing her contact-lenses. 'I know it's terribly extravagant but I do adore caviare *blinis*. Am I going to let myself be tempted?' She smiled winsomely at Luigi. 'Well, yes, I think I am. The *blinis* to start with, Luigi. And then . . . and then . . .' She peered even more closely at the menu, her eyes beginning to squint, and at last decided: 'And a small portion – a very small portion – of the *scaloppine al limone*. You know how I hate an overloaded plate, Luigi . . .'

When Luigi had left them – Lorna's order was far more modest and she certainly would not have opted for an expensive bottle of claret, since it was unlikely that they would drink even half of it between them – Miranda puffed out her fine-spun hair with both small, plumply pink hands, gave a satisfied glance at her reflection in the gilt-framed mirror opposite her and then leant across the table to say to Lorna: 'Now, tell me all about yourself.'

'What is there to tell?' Lorna knew that when Miranda issued this command, it was only a preliminary to some lengthy confidence of her own. 'Life goes on as usual. Things happen to my patients – I don't mean only things like births and deaths and illnesses but also all those emotional and spiritual crises that would once have been confided to the parish priest. But to me, well, nothing ever seems to happen. Matty says I should be thankful for that. Happy the country without a history, happy the person without a history. But sometimes I find myself wishing . . .'

'Well, don't! That cripple woman's right – as usual. Too much happens to me, far too much. I suppose that's what comes of being married to a man like Brian . . . Thank you, Dino.' Miranda always took the trouble to learn the names of the waiters at the restaurants that she frequented, just as she also knew the names of the people who habitually served her at Harrods. It was not that she cared about them: but she had found that that way she got quicker and better service. She put a forkful of *blinis* into her mouth. Long ago, when she and Lorna had been at school together, her teeth had been crooked and widely spaced apart; but 'this wonderful Austrian in Harley Street' had put that right for her soon after her marriage – at Brian's expense of course – and now the caps glistened in the glow from the lamp beside her. 'Mmm. Absolutely delicious. You were a fool to choose that dreary avocado. One should never eat out what one can prepare oneself at home. I've told you that a thousand times.'

Miranda began to talk of Brian. There had been this, well, this gradual lack of interest. It could be his work of course – the market was behaving in an absolutely catastrophic way, thanks to these wretched Arabs and even more wretched miners. But on the other hand . . . She was always suspicious when he started to be too generous. Lorna would remember that time when the gifts were just showering down like confetti and all the time he was having if off with that little slut of an *au pair* from Helsinki. Oh, there was something going on all right, of that she was certain. But quite what it was . . .

Lorna suddenly felt the impulse to be brutal to this pampered, greedy, overdressed woman opposite to her. Yes, they were close friends, they would probably always be close friends; but really she hated her and for a short while over that lunch in the dimly lit, exorbitantly expensive restaurant she realized that she hated her. 'Would you really care if there were someone else?'

'Well, darling, of course I should! What an odd question to ask! I'm not in love with him any longer – after all these years it would be incredible if I were – but I *am* very fond of him. And I should hate to lose him. He's always been very good to me, you know,' she said in a soft, pensive voice; and at once all memory of that brief realization of her hatred of this 'friend' was erased from Lorna's consciousness in an access of pity. 'I don't just mean material things. When I had that ghastly op – well, no one could have been sweeter or more understanding. And he was *worried*, desperately worried.' She gave a little shudder, though the restaurant was in fact over-heated, as she pushed her half-emptied plate away from her. Then she reached into her bag for a cigarette. Lorna hated it when the acrid smoke of a Turkish cigarette was blown across her food; but in all the years that they had eaten meals together she had never once protested. 'Oh, it would be terrible if I lost him.'

'You won't lose him. He's far too fond of you. And far too fond of the children. If there *is* something – and probably it's only in your imagination – well, it's just something like that business with that Finnish girl. I'm certain of that.'

Again the small, plumply pink hands – a diamond on one of them caught the light as previously the capped teeth had done – fluffed the fine, *bouffant* hair that made a bell-like cocoon round the complacent, unlined face. All at once Miranda giggled. 'And yet you know, Lorna, although I'm so fond of him – and though it would kill me, yes, literally kill me to lose him – there are moments when I think to myself how exciting it would be to have some little hole-in-the-corner affair of my own. Is that very shocking?'

Lorna shook her head, wondering if it shocked her or not. No, not really. Miranda had had many little hole-in-the-corner affairs in the early years of her marriage.

'I want someone before I get too old for it – before it becomes undignified and makes people laugh at me. Someone like Dino,' she added mischievously, eyeing the waiter, who at that moment was pushing the sweet-trolley past them. The trousers were stretched tight across his buttocks. 'An Italian would be enormously exciting.'

'Oh, Miranda, how *could* you?' Lorna found herself giggling too, in a shameful way that she only did with this one woman friend of hers.

'He's very handsome. And I adore his behind! I'm sure he'd oblige. If one made it worth his while of course. There was this ancient old girl in our hotel in Corfu last autumn – an American dowager who must have been at least a hundred, very grand, very *comme il faut* – and Brian learned from the manager that she was just running through the waiters one after another, one after another. The manager was full of admiration for her – and for the waiters, too, who were making a pretty packet. Sometimes I feel I'd like to let myself go like that. Make a real pig of myself. Don't you? No, of course you don't. Oh, Lorna, you're so *admirable*!' She managed to make the epithet sound pejorative. 'Anyway, if I can't ask Dino for anything else, at least I'm going to ask him for some of those super strawberries. Where do you suppose they come from?'

When Miranda had her strawberries before her – Lorna had ordered only coffee – she leant across the table and said in a soft, sibilant voice: 'But even more than Dino, I must confess to you, my dear, that the person I've always *longed* to get to bed is your dear, elusive Bob.'

'*Bob!*'

'Don't sound so amazed. He's terribly attractive. And he has that remoteness that paradoxically becomes a kind of come-on for me. Oh, yes, I'd love to get him to bed. I've been crazy about him ever since I first met him with you at that ghastly party in Islington. Do you remember it?'

Lorna nodded. Since someone had managed to be sick on her coat, where she had left it across a sagging bed in a dank, ill-lit bedroom, she could hardly have forgotten it.

Miranda sighed. 'But I never seem to get anywhere with him, however hard I try. I don't honestly think he likes me.' She popped a strawberry into her mouth and sucked on it, as though it were a sweet. 'Does he?'

'Oh, of course he does.'

'No, dear, you must say that with more conviction if you want me to believe it. I've done all I can but really it's obvious. Even Brian has noticed and you know how little *he* takes in – if it's not to do with business.'

'Bob often says how much he likes you both,' Lorna lied. 'He's not demonstrative. It's not his way.'

'He does everything possible to avoid us. We must have asked him round with you at least a dozen times this past year and he's come only once – and that was to a cocktail-party . . . My only way of consoling myself' – she popped another strawberry into her mouth and again sucked – 'is to tell myself that probably he just doesn't like *any* woman.'

'What do you mean?'

'Well, dear, a man doesn't have to lisp or peroxide his hair in order to prefer his own kind. We've all learned *that* these last few years. Haven't we?' Lorna was staring at her with such concentrated intensity, not into her eyes but at the mouth out of which these words had come, that she gave a short, nervous laugh that was almost a gulp. 'I've not upset you, have I?'

'I've never heard anything so – so crazy.'

An extraordinary blush began to mount up Lorna's throat, to spread across her cheeks and finally reach her forehead.

'I was only joking,' Miranda said hurriedly. 'I didn't really mean it. After all, it's not as though he were particularly friendly with any man. Is it? Don't take me seriously.'

'I think I'll have some more coffee,' Lorna said, looking round her shoulder for Dino.

'You should have had some of these strawbugs. Marvellous!'

Both women had suddenly become diffident and graceless in each other's company and it was not long before Lorna said. 'Well, I suppose I'd better get started on my rounds.'

'Oh, not so soon!' But the protest carried no conviction.

When, smiling unctuously, Dino had brought the bill, Miranda drew the plate towards her, placed a ten-pound note on it and said: 'I suppose we'd better leave him all the change. After all, he *was* very solicitous. And he has got that gorgeous behind!'

'What do I owe you?'

Miranda replied, as Lorna had known from experience that she would: 'Well, don't let's quibble. We might as well go fifty-fifty.'

Lorna slipped a five-pound note across the table.

'We must do this again soon. I *have* so enjoyed it.'

Driving back from Knightsbridge to Parson's Green, Lorna went over all that Miranda had said about Bob. *A man doesn't have to have a lisp and peroxide his hair in order to prefer his own kind.* And perhaps his own kind had once been that servant who had been so gentle with the needle and was now – well, why not? – Harry Van Fleet. There was that patient of hers, a long-distance lorry-driver, heavily tattooed and heavily moustached, who had come to her some months ago with non-specific urethritis. Wholly unembarrassed and unselfconscious, he had speculated whether he might not have been infected by a boy he had picked up on the Ramblas in Barcelona. She had had other similar patients, not only male but female, who had been similarly frank. If, as Miranda had said, Bob had never had any close man-friend – or, at least, none of whom she knew – it was equally true that he had never had any close woman-friend.

Minutes later she was taking the blood-pressure of the elderly countess in the foetid basement flat.

'This is not necessary, my dear! It is not necessary! What is the point of it? You know and I know that my blood-pressure is too high and that my heart is too weak and that soon – next week or maybe tomorrow – you will no longer have to visit me. Let us leave all this and have a cup of tea and a little chat. Yes?'

Lorna shook her head, frowned and continued to pump, hardly taking in what the Polish woman was saying. Over and over, over and over, she could hear Miranda's voice: *A man doesn't have to have a lisp and peroxide his hair in order to prefer his own kind ...*

18

'God, what an evening!'

'What on earth have you been doing? I thought you'd be back long before me.'

'Watching someone die.' Lorna shivered, partly from the rawness of the February night, still icy on her lips and forehead as she held her hands out, chilblains itching, to the grudging warmth of the paraffin stove, and partly from the memory of a scene she wanted to forget. 'A child.'

'A *child*!'

She nodded. 'Don't let's talk about it. One's always being told that we doctors are callous – we have to be callous or else we couldn't carry on. And then something – something suddenly . . .' Again she shivered. 'I need a cup of tea. Or, better still a drink.'

'Have both. You get the tea and I'll get the drink for you. I was just having one myself.'

Suddenly she became aware of the contrast between her dejection and her brother's exaltation. His eyes were shining, his cheeks had a rosy flush and, as he talked to her, he bounced slightly up and down on the balls of his feet.

As she poured the water out of the electric kettle into the teapot, she asked: 'And what sort of evening did you have?'

'Oh, this bloke and I had a couple of drinks together.'

'Where?'

'In that pub on that corner at South Kensington.'

'Which corner?' she wanted to ask; but then she suddenly noticed the long scratch down one side of his neck, from his left ear to the edge of his collar. 'What's that?' She pointed.

A hand moved up to the laceration and the forefinger ran along it, as though until that moment he had not been aware that it was there. 'Oh, that!' He shrugged. 'I fell off the motorbike.' Only a few weeks before he had bought a second-hand Honda – to the relief of Lorna, who had long since wearied of lending him the car when she badly needed it herself.

Did one receive a scratch like that from a fall? Well, it was possible, she supposed.

'You should put some iodine on it. It looks rather nasty.'

'Iodine will only make it look even nastier.' He sipped at his whisky-and-soda, his free hand once more going to the scratch. 'It's nothing much. Until you mentioned it, I didn't know it was there.'

'You must have felt it.'

'No, truly, not . . .' He perched on the edge of the kitchen table, at which she was seated. 'Now tell me about this child.'

She shook her head vigorously. 'No, Bob. No! I told you. I don't want to talk about it.'

'Was it a boy or a girl?'

'I don't want to talk about it.'

'But just tell me that.'

'I don't want to talk about it.'

It was on Wednesdays that the dustmen called or, more accurately, were supposed to call. Tomorrow would be Wednesday and as she filled her hot-water bottle – Bob had by then gone upstairs, singing to himself in his light, not unattractive tenor ('A room with a view, *And* you . . .') – Lorna wondered if he had remembered to put out the bags. Long ago the dustmen had refused to fetch them from the yard at the side of the house; then in recent months they had even taken to ignoring them if they were left in the basement. 'I can't lug those things around,' Mrs Emerson had said. 'They're too much for me.' And so the task had fallen to Bob, who usually forgot to do it.

Well, she'd better remind him before he got undressed. Though they usually arrived late in the afternoon, the dustmen had a way of turning up at cockcrow on precisely those mornings when the bags were not yet out. But then, peering through the window Lorna saw that, by a miracle, Bob had, for once, remembered.

Clutching her hot-water bottle to herself with both hands as she mounted the stairs, she called out to him: 'Thanks for putting out the bags.'

'Well, it's Wednesday tomorrow, isn't it?'

'As the bags are out, this'll probably be a week when they either come to us at the end of their round or decide not to come at all.'

'Perhaps I should put some iodine on this scratch after all.'

'Yes, I think you should. You don't want it to go septic.'

He appeared, jacket and tie off, in his bedroom doorway:

'Have you got some iodine?'

'In the bathroom cupboard. I'd better do it for you.'

'No, no! I can get it! And I can put it on! For God's sake . . .'

I mustn't fuss over him, she told herself. He's too old for it now. He no longer likes it.

'There's cotton-wool there, too,' she said, passing on to her own bedroom.

The next afternoon the dustmen had still not called. The two bags, made of a filmy grey plastic, lay slumped against the railings by the gate, a recent shower of rain causing them to glisten where the water had collected in their folds. Perhaps it was not only rain that glistened there – only the previous week one of the dustmen, the backs of his swollen hands heavily tattooed, had shouted at her as she emerged from the house: 'Some dog 'as gone and bloody well pissed all over this bag of yours!'

Since one of the bags was barely half-full, Lorna decided that she might as well add to it the overflowing contents of the pedal-bin in the kitchen. She struggled with the knot, her fingernails slipping on the plastic – yes, she hoped that the moisture was only rain – and at last succeeded in undoing it and jerking the neck open. Later she was often to wonder what had then made her pause and peer into its depths rather than at once tip out the contents of the pedal-bin beside her. There was, in addition to the usual detritus of potato-peelings, tea-leaves, tin cans, newspapers and wrappings, a Marks & Spencer's bag which had been neatly secured at its neck with a piece of string. Bob would often bring down the contents of the waste-paper basket in his room in some such bag but the tying of the string around the neck was new.

On an impulse she stooped, heaved up this bag and then, fingers trembling, unfastened the string. Inside were fragments of letters, torn into pieces so small that it was impossible to learn anything from them – there was nothing uncommon in that – the carton in which a bottle of after-shave lotion had been packaged, a copy of *The Times* several days old and another, even older, of the *New Statesman*, and then, at the bottom of all, a shirt. She recognized this shirt immediately as being the one which she had given him on his recent birthday; and she also thought – could she be sure? – that he had been wearing it when he had gone out the previous evening.

Now she pulled it out, hoping that no one, above all Bob, would see what she was doing. Less than two months old, it was in perfect condition - collars and cuffs unfrayed – except that down its front there were some bloodstains that had hardened and darkened, puckering the candy-stripes. She stared at these for several seconds, her mouth slightly parted as she felt the saliva gather behind her teeth; then she stuffed it back deep into the Marks & Spencer's bag, to let this bag fall back into the bigger plastic bag. With a decisive gesture she finally emptied the contents of the pedal-bin on top.

Thoughtfully, she went back up the stairs and into the house.

Bob, hearing her, called down from his room: 'How about a cup of tea? I feel parched, I don't know why. It must be this night-storage heater up here.'

'I'll make some.' She went into the kitchen, filled the kettle, began to put out the cups and saucers and plates. But as she touched all these familiar objects in turn, she still seemed to feel on her fingertips those dry, rusty encrustations on that expensive shirt.

'Any cake?' Bob had now joined her.

'Should be some in the tin.' She pointed.

'Have you finished for the day?'

'Oh God, no.'

'I thought I heard you go out and then come in again.'

'Yep. I – I thought I might as well fill that bag up before the men came. *If* they come. The rubbish bag.'

'This cake is stale.' He made a fastidious grimace, as dry crumbs scattered from his mouth to the floor.

The kettle began its high-pitched whistle.

'Hell!' Steam from it enveloped her hand.

'That's a rotten design,' he said. 'One's always scalding oneself.'

She stirred the tea-leaves round and round in the pot. Then peering down into it, she asked: 'Why on earth did you throw away that shirt?'

'What shirt?'

'The shirt I gave you for your birthday.' She had difficulty in forcing her gaze up to his; and when at last she succeeded in doing so, she noticed how pale he had gone around the nostrils and the mouth.

'I'd bled all over it. From that accident I had.'

'But blood comes out. I wish you'd told me, I could have soaked it in salt. That works as a rule, you know. It might even get the stains out now. Would you like me to –?'

'No!' The monosyllable was loud and sharp. Then he repeated more quietly: 'No. It's too late. Leave it.'

'But it's worth a try, Bob.'

'No.' He held out his cup, his hand completely steady, and, clumsily unsteady, she began to pour out into it. 'To tell you the truth, old girl, I've never been mad about that pattern, you know.'

'But you *chose* it! You came with me and chose it.'

'Did I?' He was completely cool now; there was no trace left of that brief former panic. 'Well, I made a mistake, I'm afraid.'

Lorna sipped at her scalding tea.

'You've given me some lovely shirts in the past,' he said. 'But that one – well, it somehow just wasn't me. So there's no point in your wasting time in trying to get out stains that probably won't come out in any case.'

'I could have got them out,' she pursued in a slow, sullen-sounding voice.

'Forget it!' Once again he bit into the cake and once again the crumbs scattered. 'Christ! This cake tastes of dust. Dust and ashes.'

19

Like many other of Lorna's elderly patients, the Polish woman had become obsessed with the state of her bowels. Her faltering heart, the rheumatism that made it an agony for her even to cross the room to open the front door of the cluttered, den-like basement flat, the blood-pressure that gave her constant headaches and what she called 'my dizzy turns': none of these things was as important to her.

Weary from an afternoon of visiting, Lorna said: 'I don't think you should worry so much about going, really I don't.'

'Worry so much about going! I am not worried about going! Why should I worry? I am ready, now, now! All my life I have been a good Catholic, all my life!' The large face that usually looked as if it had been inexpertly fashioned from tallow, began to glow with indignation. 'My husband is waiting for me, two of my sons are waiting for me. Why should I worry? I do not worry. When God wishes to take me, I am ready. Now, now!'

It was a comic and macabre misunderstanding.

Later, her battered bag heavy on her arm, Lorna heaved herself up the slippery iron steps, the February evening lying chill and moist on her forehead, cheeks and lips like some invisible cobweb, so that she put up her free hand as though to brush it away. There was one more call, the most depressing of all – to the grub, who had succumbed to some obscure urinary infection, obstinately resistant to the wide range of antibiotics that she had prescribed for him – and then there would be the warmth of her own house, the three or four cups of strong, scalding tea and the television set. Bob, filming some commercial, would probably not be home.

On the Green some children, four or five girls in skirts so short that, as they raced hither and thither, their knickers were revealed, screamed in an intensity of joy while the traffic, choked and evil-smelling, crawled around their island. From the other side of the road Lorna watched them; and suddenly some part of their wild pleasure in chasing a tennis ball through the dimming light of the evening that was descending around them, communicated itself to her also. Once the old Polish woman might have run hither and thither like that on some ancestral estate she had not seen for half a lifetime; and some day that child with the hair streaming backwards in the icy breeze ... But it was better not to think of that.

Cautiously, she began to cross the road, to balance giddily on the exiguous island in the middle of it before at last making a dash for the further pavement. She hardly noticed the large Mercedes parked along a double yellow line, so that the oncoming traffic was forced to slow and swerve around it. But then she was looking into the face at the wheel and, though there was a cap pulled down low on the forehead and a scarf came almost to the mouth, she could not fail to recognize Harry Van Fleet. Evidently this evening he had dispensed with his driver. Their eyes met and he gazed at her as she walked towards him as though she were a total stranger. Then, as she was about to walk past him and on towards the side-street in which her own car was parked, he made a small gesture of acknowledgement, raising one gloved hand from the wheel and then letting it fall back again and at the same time inclining his head slightly forward. She, too, nodded and as she did so, the electrically operated window began to glide down between them.

'Hello!' he said. 'Fancy seeing *you* here!'

It was a somewhat strange remark: Parson's Green was, after all, her own ground.

'I'm on my rounds. I have a patient on that corner.' She gestured vaguely through the mist that was beginning to descend. Chattering like starlings, the girls raced past them, their game now over. Briefly his eyes went to them.

'Oh, yes. Yes, a patient. You're a doctor, of course.'

'Are you waiting for Bob?'

'Bob? Oh, your brother, you mean! Well, no, as a matter of fact, I'm not. I'm waiting for – for someone else.'

It seemed an odd place to be waiting. She found herself wondering even then about the identity and, indeed, the reality of that someone else.

'Oh. I see. I just thought . . .'

'How *is* Bob? It's a long time since we saw each other.'

'Oh, he's fine. Fine. He's got a job today.'

'Job?'

'Filming. A commercial.'

'Oh, yes, of course. Well, that's good, isn't it? I always tell him he doesn't have enough to occupy him . . . Horrible evening, isn't it?' He shivered inside the heated car, lowering his chin yet deeper into the enveloping cashmere scarf. 'This winter just seems to go on and on and on.' He laughed, showing those white, over-large teeth. 'The winter of our discontent,' he said.

'Well, I must be going.' She, too, now gave a small shiver.

'Bob must bring you round some time.'

'Thank you.'

She walked on; and then, suddenly, she was certain that behind her the Mercedes had begun to move forward. She felt its approach with an extraordinary trepidation, as though it might mount the pavement and pounce on her, to choke out her life beneath its prodigious weight of steel. But there it was, gliding effortlessly ahead of her now; and there he was, the cap at the same jaunty angle and the scarf still concealing most of his face, as he stared out ahead of him, with no wave of acknowledgement or goodbye.

For once, Bob had arrived home early. When she entered the dark, narrow hall she could hear the sounds of water threshing and throbbing through the antiquated plumbing as he ran himself a bath.

'Lorna? Is that you, Lorna?'

Who else could it be? 'Yes, it's me,' she said, putting down her bag on the rickety chair that he had been promising to mend for weeks and weeks, and then drawing off her gloves. How horrible those chilblains looked! She glanced away from them and up to where he stood in his paisley-silk dressing-gown, his feet bare, looking down at her over the stair-rail.

'Just going to have a bath,' he said. 'A truly awful day. And only six quid to show for it.'

She put the gloves down on the hall table among a litter of unpaid bills and unanswered letters. Tomorrow was Sunday and perhaps then, God willing, she would have the time to deal with them. Beginning to slip out of her coat, she said: 'I've just run into a friend of yours.'

'A friend of mine? Who?' Was there a tremor of alarm in his voice or did she imagine that? 'Who?'

'Harry Van Fleet.'

'*Harry!*' He began to come down the stairs, drawing the dressing-gown closer about that still boyish figure of his. 'But *where*?'

'By the Green.'

'The Green!'

She nodded. 'He was parked there. On a double yellow line. Waiting for someone, he said.'

'How do you mean?'

'Well, that's what he said. Waiting for someone. I thought that perhaps he might be waiting for you. But he said no, it was – someone else.'

She found that she was enjoying creating one of these small shock-waves after another.

'Who on earth . . .?'

'I've no idea.'

'By the Green!'

'On a double yellow line.'

She began to go into the kitchen, aware that he still stood there, hands deep in the pockets of the dressing-gown and on his face an expression of amazement. She looked back over her shoulder:

'Anyway, he evidently decided to wait no longer. As I walked away from him, I saw him driving off.'

He followed her into the kitchen:

'You spoke to him?'

She nodded, as she filled the kettle at the sink.

'What about?'

'What I told you. He seemed to be as surprised to see me there as I was to see him. But after all, I *do* live in Parson's Green and he doesn't.'

He stood silent in the centre of the kitchen, his lower lip caught between his teeth and his hands still deep in the dressing-gown pockets. Then he gave a little shudder. But that could have been because it was cold in there and he was barefooted and wearing nothing beneath the dressing-gown.

'Take care that bath doesn't overflow.'

At that he gave himself a visible shake and moved towards the door. 'Yes,' he said. 'Yes.' As he went out, he said in a tone of wonder: 'By the Green! But that's extraordinary!'

20

From her bed Lorna could hear the near-groans and gasps as Matty dragged herself up the stairs. 'Matty, don't! Don't!' she cried out, her throat raw and husky. 'I can come down. I can easily come down.' She snaked across the bed for her dressing-gown and then, kneeling, thrust first one arm and then the other into it. 'Matty!'

'Perfectly all right . . . Good for me . . . Not all that difficult . . .' Each phrase seemed to be torn out of the cruelly lopsided body as Matty persevered.

'Oh, Matty! Really! I'm not all that ill!' Lorna wailed at her, half in anger and half in pity, as they came face to face in the doorway.

'Back into bed!' Matty ordered, the beads of sweat glistening on her forehead where the coarse grey hair sprang upwards. 'Bob tells me you've a temp of over a hundred and one. Go on! Back into bed!'

Lorna subsided on to one corner of the bed, suddenly dizzy, a hand to her chin. 'It's just this bug that's going the rounds.' She had said the same sentence to innumerable patients during the past week. 'Now I've copped it. But I'll be down for surgery later.'

'Nothing of the kind! You'll only be sneezing and coughing your germs on everyone. Bob! *Bob!*' Matty shouted over her shoulder. 'Where's that bag of mine?'

'Bringing it. I was just refilling Lorna's hot-water bottle at the same time.'

'You don't need your bag. I've taken codeine. There's nothing else to do.'

'I'd better sound you.'

'Oh, no, Matty. No! There's nothing really wrong with me. As I said, it's just this bug.' Lorna crawled back between the bedclothes, conscious that her teeth had started to chatter. 'But what worries me – how are you going to manage?'

'Oh, perfectly well. Now don't start worrying about that.'

'Here you are!' Bob had the bag in one hand and Lorna's hot-water bottle in the other.

'You don't have to sound me. Honestly, Matty! I'd know if there were anything on my chest.'

Matty sighed. 'Very well, pet. As you wish.'

Bob slid the hot-water bottle between the bedclothes. 'Poor Lorna,' he said.

'Poor you – having to be my nurse.'

'Now is there anything you need?' Matty asked.

'No, no! Honestly! Bob can do anything that's necessary and Mrs E. has promised to come in later. Your hands will be full enough already.'

Leaning the weight of her whole body against the side of Lorna's bed, Matty lowered a hand. 'Yes, you've certainly got a temperature. No doubt of that.' The hand moved to Lorna's wrist.

'Yes, and my pulse is quick too. It's just this bug, Matty, nothing else.'

Matty sighed, removing her fingers from Lorna's wrist and drawing in her small, rounded chin. 'Well, if there's nothing I can do for you . . .'

'The patients will be waiting,' Lorna said, suddenly feeling the impulse to burst into hysterical laughter. 'All those lovely patients. Lots and lots of them. Poor Matty!'

Matty squinted down at Lorna, faintly alarmed. 'Well, yes, I expect that the waiting-room is full.'

'Do take care on the stairs! Oh, I wish you hadn't attempted the climb!'

'I'll be back,' Bob called. 'Just let me see Matty out.'

That afternoon either the two of them played two-handed whist together or Bob, lying across the bottom of her bed, read to her from the newspaper, while she dozed intermittently. She told him that he did not have to stay with her all the time; that she was perfectly all right on her own; that he must go out and not worry about her. But during that day and the two days that followed he rarely left her except to sleep, to prepare the meals that they ate together in the sickroom or to rush out to do some shopping. At first she was touched by so much loving attention, looking gratefully into his face as he brought a wash-basin to her bedside and insisted on himself washing first one of her hands and then the other with what she had not the heart to tell him was not, in fact, her flannel but the cloth that Mrs Emerson used for the bath. But then his constant presence, lying across the bed or outstretched in the armchair by the fire, started to become a burden. She no longer wanted him to hold the cup of tea to her lips; to help her into her dressing-gown when she had to go to the lavatory; to go through this incessant ritual of puffing up pillows that did not need puffing up, of taking her temperature at four-hourly intervals, of labouring up and down the stairs with trays of food for which she had no appetite.

'I'm sure you've things you want to do.'

'Nothing at all! There's no film-work and it's raining outside.' He was like some large, satisfied cat as he lay stretched across the bottom of the double bed.

'And you're breathing in all my germs all the time.'

'I never catch 'flu. Remember? I've never had it. I must have some kind of lucky immunity. And anyway, if I *were* going to get it, the germs would all be at work on me by now.'

'There's that concert I can listen to. I'll be quite happy on my own.'

'But I want to listen to it too.'

'You're very good to me, Bob.' But she felt resentment growing within her, almost as though it were yet another symptom of the virus that brought on these alternate sweats and chills and made her throat and the back of her nose feel as though they were on fire.

'Not as good as you've been to me for years and years and years.'

She shifted uncomfortably at that declaration and at once there he was again at his task of plumping up her pillows and tugging at her sheets. 'I can see you've got yourself into a mess again.' He looked at his watch when he had finished. 'Time for your next dose of codeine.'

'Oh, Bob! Please! Please go out!'

Then on the third day, when her temperature had fallen and a depression had begun to envelop her like the mist that had enveloped the trees in the garden beyond her window, all at once he was restless. With the hyperaesthesia of illness, she had sensed the oncoming of this restlessness long before there had been any overt signs, so that two or three times she had repeated her urgings that he must really get out and cease to bother about her until, angry, he had shouted at her, 'Oh, for God's sake, Lorna! I've told you! There's nothing for me to do, there's nothing, absolutely nothing I want to do.'

But soon after that outburst he had started to get off the bed and wander to the window, looking out into the mist enshrouding the narrow, barren garden, while one hand fiddled with the screw of the burglar-lock. He would then eventually turn back to Lorna and the high bed with a sigh and a rueful shrug of the shoulders. 'What an afternoon!' he exclaimed more than once. 'You're lucky to be tucked up safely in bed.'

Finally, when he had gone for the fourth time to the window, standing there, on this occasion, for minutes on end, his forehead pressed against one of the panes while, once more, his fingers fiddled with that lock, Lorna risked a renewal of his displeasure and said: 'Oh, do go out, Bob! Please! It's awful for you to be cooped up here with me all this time.'

He hesitated, looking back and forth between her on the bed and the trees in the murk outside the window, as though he were summing up some kind of choice. Then he said with an assumed reluctance (she could see that really he was relieved), 'Well, if you're so eager to get rid of me for a while . . .'

'It's not that. But it's not fair to expect you to –'

'Yes, I know, I know. Well, perhaps I'll take myself out for a moment or two. As a matter of fact' – it was as if only then had the remembrance come to him – 'I did say to this friend that I might look in for a drink.'

'Yes, do that.'

'You're sure you can do without me?'

'Quite sure ... In any case, Mrs E. should be coming up at any moment. If she keeps her promise.'

'Well, in that case ...' As he went over to the door his step had become suddenly lighter, the swing of his arms and the carriage of his head had become more jaunty. He paused, fingers on the door-handle: 'All right if I take the car?'

'Oh, yes, of course. I'll hardly be needing it!'

She heard him race down the stairs, taking them in twos and threes.

'There's no point my doing out this room until you're up and about again,' Mrs Emerson announced on her arrival, without asking Lorna how she felt or if there were anything she needed. 'Whew – there's a right old fug in here!' she added. 'Look at them window-panes. You've got them all steamed up.'

Lorna had noticed that though, to their faces, Mrs Emerson was usually quick to sympathize with the illnesses, real or imaginary, of the patients – tut-tutting and sighing over their enumerations of their symptoms and even herself attempting a rudimentary diagnosis while they were still in the waiting-room – any other illness, whether upstairs or in her own family, made her adopt a brusque, hectoring tone.

'Yes, it is rather warm.'

'I shouldn't have thought you'd need that fire on. Not being in bed and all.'

'I get these shivering attacks.'

'Well, that's all part of the 'flu, isn't it? That's nothing to do with whether there's a fire on or not, now is it?'

She crossed over to the gas fire as though to turn if off. But Lorna said: 'I'd like it left on.'

'As you wish. It's you that'll have to foot the bill.' Duster in hand, Mrs Emerson swivelled round and peered at her. 'You don't *look* all that ill. Your colour's good.'

'Well, I'm glad to hear that. I still feel ghastly.'

'You don't want to brood. That's the worst thing when you've got a touch of 'flu.' Again she surveyed Lorna: 'No, I shouldn't have said you looked at all bad really. My old man was as white as paper when he had his go. But it was all I could do to keep him in bed for just a day . . . That tray needs taking down.'

'Yes, could you be an angel and take it down for me? My brother forgot it.'

Mrs Emerson squinted down indignantly into the dregs in the cup on the tray that she had now retrieved. 'You shouldn't be drinking coffee. Tea's the thing for you. Or orange juice. Not coffee.'

'I felt I wanted a change from endless cups of tea.'

'Well, it's your choice, I suppose.' She made for the door, massive shoulders bowed as though the tray were heavily loaded. 'So he's out,' she said. 'Mr Ambler.'

'Yes, he's gone out for a little. I persuaded him.'

'Dr Spencer said he'd been sitting up here with you all the day. And he was up here all yesterday too, wasn't he?'

'Yes. He's been very good. I tried to persuade him to go out but he wouldn't hear of it.'

'Well, that's daft.' Mrs Emerson sniffed, as she manoeuvred the tray around the door. 'It's not as though there were anything *seriously* wrong with you . . . I mean, it's not healthy, is it? Not healthy at all . . . Well, give us a call if you need anything. I'll give the sitting-room a quick going over and try to clear up some of that mess he's made in the kitchen.'

As Mrs Emerson thudded down the stairs, Lorna lay back on the pillows, eyes shut and hands gripping the sheet that lay, damp and hot, across her throat. *I mean it's not healthy, is it?* . . . The words seemed to carry a disturbing suggestiveness. From time to time in the past Lorna had sensed that, like Matty, Mrs Emerson disapproved of the closeness and exclusiveness of the relationship between herself and Bob. But surely that could not be what she had meant now? Surely she had meant only that it was bad for him to stay cooped up in a sickroom day after day?

From downstairs there came a crash, followed by a loud 'Bugger!' Evidently something had been broken; but what it was she would never learn from Mrs Emerson. Later she would either see for herself or Bob would report the disaster to her.

21

'Be an angel and rub some of this muck on my back.'

'I'll do it,' Brian said. 'Give me the bottle.' He had joined Miranda and Lorna in Agadir for the second and final week of Lorna's convalescence.

'When Brian's as solicitous as this, I know that he's been up to something in my absence,' Miranda murmured, rolling over on to her stomach.

'Oh, balls!' His vehemence suggested guilt to Lorna. 'I've been far too busy this last week to think of anything but work.'

Lorna hugged her bare knees, staring out to where a group of Germans – an elderly man kippered by the sun, two young girls and a thin, effeminate-looking boy – were splashing intrepidly in the sea. There were six more days to go and already she was fretting to be back.

'Isn't it incredible?' Miranda murmured sensuously, head turned sideways on the towel while the powerful hands kneaded at her shoulders. 'I bet that waiting-room of yours is full of patients coughing and sneezing their heads off and here are we out on this beach in brilliant sunshine.'

Lorna sighed.

'Aren't you enjoying yourself?' Brian asked, cupping his hand and tilting the bottle into it.

'Oh, yes, of course I am!' It was Brian who had insisted on paying for her to come away with Miranda to recuperate. 'It's just . . .'

'Just what?' Miranda prompted.

'Oh, the thought of those wretched patients. And of Matty too, of course.'

'She's got that locum, hasn't she?'

Lorna nodded.

'Well then?' Brian said.

'He's such a *boy*. And not awfully competent. He's got virtually no experience and I don't think he's really interested in anything except his rugger.'

'Oh, he and Matty will manage all right together. She always strikes me as extremely able in spite of being a cripple . . . How's that, darling?'

Miranda sat up: 'Lovely.' Then, with a voluptuous gesture, as though she were beckoning 'Come, come, come!' to some invisible lover, she held out her hands, arms fully extended, towards the sun, wriggling her torso as she did so. 'One can't always be thinking of others,' she said. 'You have to think of yourself. You were thoroughly pulled down after that long bout of 'flu.'

'If you'd gone back to work at once, the likelihood is that you'd only have had a relapse,' Brian took up. His squat, muscular body, with the grey hair thick on his chest and even between his shoulder-blades, had been burned to the colour of terra-cotta. That night he would suffer.

Suddenly Miranda said: 'It's not Bob, is it?' She turned to Lorna, head on one side as one hand played with a lock of ashen hair.

'Bob?'

'It's not him that you're worrying about?'

'Of course not.'

'I bet it is! I bet you're far more worried about him than about any of those patients or poor old Matty!'

'Oh, don't be silly! Bob's well able to look after himself.'

'Of course he is, my dear. But you just won't believe it.'

Lorna said nothing, frowning down at the fingers with which she was now scooping up sand to make a castle.

'Bob's a grown man,' Brian took up, as though he and Miranda had planned a concerted attack on her between them. 'You mustn't expect him to be tied to your apron-strings for ever.'

'He's never been tied to my apron-strings – as you put it.' The other two realized, from the sudden iciness of her tone, that they had gone too far with her and Miranda sniggered nervously as Lorna waited for her to say her usual 'It's all a *joke*, darling. Can't you take a joke? What's happened to your sense of humour?' But it was Brian who answered:

'You must admit the two of you are far closer to each other than the majority of brothers and sisters.'

'I don't know about the majority of brothers and sisters. We're certainly good friends, we've always been good friends. But he leads his own life, I lead mine. I don't think there's anything very odd about our relationship.'

'Not *odd*, dear. We didn't mean that. But, well, I wonder if all that proximity . . .' Again Miranda extended her plump, dimpled arms to the sun, this time with her eyes shut. Her lips began to part as though she were on the verge of smiling to that invisible lover radiating his warmth down upon her.

'It's convenient for us to live together. Life would be pretty lonely for me otherwise. And Bob couldn't afford on what he earns . . .' But why the hell should she be justifying the whole relationship to these two busybodies? She began to get to her feet, dusting the sand off her legs and shoulders with her towel. 'I'm getting rather cold,' she said. 'I think I'll walk back to my room and get into something warmer.'

'*Cold*, darling! But it's baking out here.'

Lorna began to walk away from them, her eyes fixed on the elderly, shrunken German, who was now wrestling in the water with one of the two squealing girls, while the young man, bony arms crossed over bony chest, looked on disconsolately.

22

All three of them were slightly tipsy from the champagne they had been swilling in the first-class section of the aeroplane. Miranda drew her fur coat closer around her as they waited interminably for their baggage.

'Christ! Isn't it marvellous to be back in dear old Blighty? There's no place like home – thank God!' Draughts snaked over the floor and the lights were so dim that the Customs Hall had become a vast, echoing cavern. 'This is like some anteroom to hell.'

'Well, yes, I agree that there's a lot to be said for a country like Morocco where the poor and the underprivileged still set their demands so low. A little begging, a little pilfering, a little baksheesh ... Who cares if one loses the hub caps of a car or a thermos flask?' (In Agadir they had lost both on an excursion.) 'At least they leave one the clothes on one's back and most of the money in one's wallet.' Brian took a hip-flask from the pocket of his overcoat and gulped from it. 'Lorna?'

She shook her head.

'What can they be *doing* with our luggage?' Miranda demanded. 'D'you think there's been another strike of which we haven't heard?'

At long last they emerged – Brian had even succeeded in finding a man who was prepared to wheel their suitcases for them – and there, to Lorna's astonishment, was Bob waiting for her, in his beige cashmere coat with a long silk scarf trailing one end over a shoulder.

'Bob! You shouldn't have bothered. And we're hours and hours late.'

'Oh, I love wandering about an airport. You see the oddest sights. There was this covey – a whole harem of them – of women

113

in yashmaks or whatever they call those things, huddled over there' – he pointed into a gloomy recess – 'sucking Coca-Cola out of bottles with straws. And at least half a dozen dark, sinister-looking men who are obviously potential hi-jackers.' He was in the highest of spirits, even kissing Miranda affectionately, both arms around her, instead of giving her his usual peck.

'But we were going to drive Lorna back. I left the car in the car-park here. No difficulty at all.' Lorna could smell the whisky from the flask on Brian's breath as he leant across her, one hand on her shoulder, more for his own support than for her protection.

'You all look marvellous,' Bob said.

'I feel a total wreck. Oh, how grim it all seems!' But some of Bob's exhilaration seemed to have communicated itself to Miranda. She no longer looked so disconsolate and her voice had lost its peevish, spoiled-child tone.

In the car – Lorna noticed how filthy Bob had allowed it to get, both outside and in – brother and sister smiled at each other in a sudden access of happiness at being together once again, as they watched Brian reverse the Triumph and then, with a wave of the hand, screech away in it.

'He'll be lucky if he isn't picked up by the police. He seems pretty cut.'

'Oh, Brian always drives best when he's drunk,' Lorna laughed, again from the sheer happiness that continued to well up within her. 'Just as Miranda always maintains that he makes love best when he's drunk.'

'He's the sort of person who ought to be drunk all the time . . . Good to see you, Lorna.' The car began to move out on to the motorway.

'What's the news?'

'Oh, nothing very startling. You've seen the papers I imagine. Things just drift from bad to worse.'

'I didn't mean that sort of news. I mean the news of you and the house and Matty.'

'Well, that's all also pretty dreary. Matty and Mrs E. were determined to mother me from the moment that you left. There was an amusing change in their attitude. You know how, when you're there, they really hate my guts. But with you away . . . Mrs E. even brought me a ghastly steak-and-kidney pie she'd cooked for my Sunday lunch. I had to throw it away. I only hope she didn't find it in the bin.'

Momentarily, Lorna thought of the shirt that he had also had to throw away; then she put that memory from her.

'Matty was always shouting up from the basement – or ringing at the bell. It became rather a bore. Once I felt that I must really offer her a drink and another time she arrived while I was having a cup of tea, so I had to offer her a cup too.'

'And the work?'

'Oh, she seems to have coped with that all right. I don't think that that muscle-bound bone-head was much use to her. But the patients seemed to like him. They usually *do* like a male doctor who's young and attractive. If it's a young and attractive female doctor, then it's another story, isn't it?'

'I wouldn't know.'

'Of course you know. I remember how, when you started, none of the patients wanted to be seen by you. Though you were far better, even then, than either Dada or Alfred.'

'Have you had a lot of lovely jobs?'

He shook his head. 'No. Just a few miserable ones. Badly paid. In small, draughty studios in the most inaccessible corners of London.'

'But the car has been a help?'

'Oh, yes, a great help. I shouldn't have fancied going out to a job early in the morning on the motorbike in this kind of weather.' He took a gloved hand off the steering-wheel and placed it briefly on her knee. 'Was Agadir fun?'

'Not bad.'

'But not really fun. Yes, I know.'

'I wish you'd been there too.'

'Brian didn't offer to pay for *me*.'

'Perhaps if you were nicer to Miranda . . .'

'Oh, I do my best.' He laughed. 'But middle-aged, sophisticated, pampered women have never really been my thing. Have they?'

'I don't really know what your *thing* is.' If she had not drunk so much on the aeroplane, she probably would not have said it.

He laughed. 'You ought to by now. My tastes are quite conventional. I like them young. And beautiful. And rich. And clever.' As he enumerated each quality, he tapped lightly with one gloved hand on the wheel.

'I suppose that's why you never find anyone who really satisfies you. You want too much.'

'Don't we all?'

As though she were being whirled round and round in a sudden dizzying eddy – yes, she had certainly drunk far too much of that champagne, gulping it down each time that Brian's strong, hairy hand had extended the bottle – she said, looking straight ahead of her out on to the gleaming motorway: 'Tell me, Bob ... Tell me ...'

'Yes?'

'Tell me. Do you think there's anything – anything *odd* about the relationship between us?'

'Odd? How do you mean?' He sounded faintly alarmed.

'Well ... Miranda and Brian – and Matty – and even Mrs E. All seem to feel ...'

'Who the hell cares *what* they think?' Now the faint alarm had become a positive anger.

Lorna continued to stare in silence at the road slipping away beneath their wheels.

'We're not the first brother and sister who are good friends – understand each other – live together ... What's *odd* about that? No one thought the Lambs odd or the Wordsworths odd. I mean, Mary Lamb was odd, bloody odd, but their actual relationship ...'

'I just don't know why they go on and on about it.'

'Don't you? *I* do. Jealousy and envy are not the rarest of human emotions, are they?'

'But why should they be jealous and envious of *us*?'

'Why? Because we've got this perfect thing between us. Better than anything they've got. Matty hasn't got the same kind of relationship with that hag of a mother of hers, not by a long chalk.

And Miranda and Brian only hang together because it would be even more of a bore for them if they were to separate. As for Mrs E. – well, who'd want to live with Mr E.? I ask you!'

'Yes, I suppose you're right.' She would have been satisfied; but somehow, racing along the motorway through the icy night, she was not so.

'Of course I'm right.'

'I think even Edie . . .' she began.

'Oh, I know that Edie resents me. You don't have to tell me. But that's because she wants an ever-loving, ever-forgiving, ever-indulgent mum entirely to her grabbing little self.' Suddenly he was speaking, not with his previous derision, but with real venom. Lorna recoiled. He had never used that tone before of Edie.

'Did she call round?'

'No. I'm glad to say.'

'Bob!'

'Well, there's no point in pretending that she and I have a lovely relationship together. Once perhaps. But not now.'

'I wish I knew what went wrong between you.'

'Nothing went wrong between us.' He turned his face to her, the lips drawn back in a way that revealed not merely his upper teeth but also the gums above them. 'Get that into your head. Nothing went wrong between us. *Nothing*.' His hands gripped the wheel as the car began to gather speed and more speed.

'Bob!' she cried out in alarm. 'Do be careful! This road is slippery.'

At that he began to slow again. In a suddenly calm voice he said: 'Edie and I could, I suppose, be described as incompatible. It's sad but there it is. Matty and I are also incompatible – not surprisingly since she's had this crush on you for years and years and years – but Matty is rather more mature and at least she tries to keep up a pretence of not actually loathing my guts . . . But Edie – well, she's at that age when pretences are just too much trouble.'

'Oh, I'm sure she really –'

'Anyway, what on earth are we discussing all these dreary people for on the day of your home-coming?' His high spirits had returned as abruptly and mysteriously as they had evaporated. Again the gloved hand patted her knee. 'Good old Lorna.'

'But one of those so-called dreary people of yours is my *daughter*!' Lorna all but cried out; but she thought better of it.

'I've got a bottle of champagne in the fridge to celebrate.'

'Oh, not champagne! Not more champagne!'

She began to laugh on a note of rising hysteria and eventually he, too, began to laugh with her.

23

The house was filthy.

'What on earth has Mrs E. been *doing* all this time?' Lorna cried out, not on the evening of her return – she was too happy then – but the next day as she faced the prospect of morning surgery with a headache that throbbed between the eyes and a feeling of overmastering lethargy. Bob merely shrugged.

Leaving her half-finished cup of tea, she jumped to her feet as much in exasperation against him as against negligent, sluttish Mrs Emerson, and began to attempt to put one of the kitchen shelves, a jumble of provisions and crockery, into some sort of order. Anna, the Siamese, who was looking a wraith – had no one bothered to feed her? – wound herself round her legs, emitting one piteous squawk after another. A packet of castor sugar slipped from her grasp and the granules showered on to the cat and the floor. 'Oh, fuck!'

'There's no need to do that now. Why not finish your breakfast?'

'Because I can't eat – I just haven't any stomach for food – when I'm surrounded by this bloody *mess*.'

'It's not so bad,' he said in a maddeningly unruffled tone, turning over a sheet of *The Times* and then biting into the slice of toast that he held in the other hand.

'It's just *awful*!'

But at that she stopped.

Later, going out on her rounds, she felt the same mingling of exasperation and despair when she viewed the state of the car in daylight. But this time there was no Mrs Emerson to blame. As she surveyed an interior choked with used tissues, cigarette-ends, sweet-papers and days-old newspapers, she found herself actually hating Bob for a few brief moments. God, the slob, the slob!

Home again from the surgery, though her back was aching now

and she realized, irritably, that her period was imminent, she decided that she would have to clean out the car there and then. If she asked – or told – Bob to do it, she knew, oh she knew so well, exactly what his answer would be. 'It's almost dark now. Don't be so idiotic. It can wait another day.' And it would wait not merely another day but a whole succession of days.

In the sitting-room she could hear the television set as he listened to yet another news bulletin. A plane had been hijacked and now, a storm-tossed bird seeking some rock on which to land, it was zigzagging across the Mediterranean in search of an aerodrome not closed to it ... But she did not care, she was not interested in the fate of the plane and its terrified hostages. All she wanted was to get that bloody car clean.

'Lorna?'

'Yes. It's me. Home.' Once again she thought: who else could it be?

She got out dust-pan and brush, her back seeming to creak painfully as though on a hinge, as she stooped to fetch it from beneath the sink.

'Where are you going?'

She did not answer.

So many sweet-papers! Angrily she swept them up into the pan. His diabetes did not allow him to eat sweets, someone else must have eaten them. And someone else must also have smoked all those cigarettes, since Bob confined himself to only an occasional one after a particularly good meal. Marlboro. She inspected one butt and then another. Christ, what a job! The dust was entering into her nostrils and was now at the back of her throat. She sneezed. There were even some of those blasted sweet-papers underneath the front passenger seat. She imagined some effeminate youth alternately sucking those glacier mints and puffing cigarette after cigarette. Or perhaps there had been a number of passengers. Perhaps Harry Van Fleet had smoked the Marlboro – yes, it was easy to make a connection between him and that brand, though not between him and glacier mints – and others had sucked the sweets. Well, she would probably never know who had been all those anonymous people ferried around in the car, *her* car, damn it.

It was then that she came on the cross on its broken gold chain among the litter beneath the seat. The chain was very fine, it was easy to see how it might have got broken. The cross itself was plain and meagre. She balanced it in her palm and thought how light it was. It might almost have been made of papier mâché or of aluminium. Eventually she put it in the pocket of her coat and continued with her angry brushing.

After she had emptied and put away the dust-pan with its brush, had washed her hands and had set out some milk for Anna, she went into the sitting-room where Bob was seated, the light off, with the television flickering against the face that he held towards it. He did not look round at her entry and when she spoke it was with a brief grimace of annoyance that he turned to her. On the screen behind his head a wrecked aeroplane now smouldered. Evidently this was a news-flash.

She put her hand into her pocket, drew out the cross on its chain and dangled it before him.

'Whose is this?'

'What is it?' His eyes went back to the screen and then returned.

'A cross. On a chain. I found it in the car.'

'In the car!'

She nodded. She could see that he was disconcerted. Then he shrugged:

'I can think of at least half a dozen people who might have dropped it there.'

'And dropped all those sweet-papers and cigarette-ends,' she added laconically.

'Why on earth do you have to clean out the car *now*? You're crazy. I could have done it in the morning.'

'Yes, you could have done it.' But would you? she wanted to add. 'Anyway, there it is.' She dropped the cross and chain into his lap. 'Give it back to its rightful owner.'

'I don't even know who its rightful owner is.'

'Well, in that case, you'd better make inquiries among those half-dozen friends.'

'Look, Lorna, I'm watching the news!'

'Fine. I'm not going to disturb you any more.'

That night, the reek of paraffin was heavy on the air as Lorna made her way upstairs to bed. Was it merely an effect of her exhaustion or had a reduction in voltage caused the landing light to dim? The ache in her back was worse and, as she climbed, her calves ached with it.

'I can even *taste* this paraffin now,' she called out, as she passed Bob's door. 'We must get rid of that stove and have a night-storage heater downstairs too.' He did not answer. 'Bob?' she said through the crack.

'Yes, I heard you. And I can smell the parafin. As a matter of fact I find it rather cosy. Comforting. I've always associated that smell with this house – for as long as I remember.'

'What are you doing?'

'Getting ready for bed. And giving myself an injection.'

'Do you want me to do it?'

'Do you want to do it?'

'I'll do it if you like.'

'Well, you know how I hate jabbing the beastly thing into my own flesh.'

'May I come in?'

'Why not?'

He was seated, shivering, in his underclothes on the edge of his bed, his hands grasped between his knees and his shoulders hunched.

'What's the matter?'

'Nothing. Thinking. That's all.'

She began to prepare the syringe, the cold and her tiredness making her maladroit and slow.

'You're done in.'

'Oh, I'll be all right after a good night's sleep.'

'You're a great believer in a good night's sleep, aren't you? But I hate the night.' He shivered more violently and stretched his naked legs out to the grudging warmth of the gas fire. 'I wish one didn't have to sleep.'

'Behind?'

'Yes, behind.'

Once again he rolled over, tugging down his pants, and once again there was that sharp intake of breath as the needle struck home.

'I nearly had a coma while you were away,' he said in a thoughtful, almost dreamy voice, slipping a hand under his pants to massage his buttock.

'Did you? Why didn't you tell me before? I suppose you forgot to inject yourself.'

'Well, I was out – away – longer than I'd expected. I was driving the car at the time.'

'Oh, Bob! But that's terribly dangerous.'

He nodded. 'I can't even remember now how I got home. But I must have done. And somehow I must have managed to get that needle into myself.'

'You could never live alone. That's what people like Matty and Miranda and Edie just don't realize. You can't look after yourself, you're not capable of it. Other diabetics can manage by themselves but you're – oh, Bob, you're *hopeless*.'

He sighed, hands once again clasped between his knees and shoulders hunched; he did not contradict her.

'You've had so many close shaves.'

'Oh, yes, I've had those!'

'Well, I suppose I'd better get along to bed. It's a heavy day tomorrow. Matty's afternoon off.'

'Yes, you need that good night's sleep of yours.' The tone was faintly mocking.

'Poor Bob.' She put a hand on his shoulder and then stooped down on an impulse and kissed him on the cheek.

He smiled up at her wanly, turning his head so that one cheekbone suddenly took fire from the gas.

'Sleep well,' he said. 'You need it. And deserve it. Happy dreams.'

But though she usually had no difficulty in dropping off as soon as her head touched the pillow, for once she could not do so. She twisted and threw herself about the bed, dislodging Anna, who let out an angry squawk as she was toppled to the floor. One moment her teeth were chattering; the next, she could feel the sweat trickle down between her breasts and break out on her forehead. Somewhere, in some drawer, there was a bottle of sleeping-pills; but though she so often prescribed them for her patients, she rarely took them herself and she had no idea where she had placed them. Deliberating whether to get out of bed and make a search, she drifted off into a state of half-sleep; and it was then that she had what was not so much a dream as a vision.

She saw the car, dusty and mud-spattered, as it had been when she had gone out to it with the pan and brush that afternoon; and she saw Bob at the wheel, in his miraculously light but warm overcoat of beige cashmere, with the long scarf trailing from his neck. Then, as though one slide had been slotted into a projector to replace another, she saw the same scene but this time with a passenger in the car: a youth as insubstantial and frail as that cross and its chain, with soft, long hair of the same tarnished gold. The chain and the cross both lay under his shirt, which was open-necked despite the cold, the two long points of its collar falling outside a pullover that was also of a fine cashmere. In close-up now she saw the two faces, Bob's and this youth's, moving towards each other and Bob's lips fastening like the suckers of some marine creature on the lips of the youth and his hands struggling and groping. The fragile chain swung up and away from the white flesh of the throat and then a link snapped. The stronger body pressed down on the weaker ...

With a twitch and a small cry she roused herself. Her heart was thudding as though she had run a race and her body was now crawling with sweat. The cat stepped delicately towards her over the eiderdown and aware of its shadow, Lorna put out a hand. Voluptuously, the cat came to it, rubbing its head, now one side and now the other, against the trembling fingers.

24

'I did what I could to help. But I don't think he was really all that grateful.'

'Oh, Matty, I'm sure he was!'

Matty shook her head as she tidied the papers on her desk. 'He wanted to be left alone. That's what he wanted. He didn't want me – or Mrs E. for that matter – fussing over him. One can't blame him. After all, he's a loner, isn't he?'

'A loner?'

'He doesn't *need* people – as you need them and as I need them. Except, of course, when he wants something from them. But that's different.'

'Oh, Matty, I wish you didn't always get him wrong. He's not like that. Really he isn't.'

'Well, anyway, he was hardly pleased on the few occasions when I tried to find out if all was well with him. In fact, after the first time that I came up the inside stairs, he went and bolted the dividing door.'

'That wasn't to keep you out, of course it wasn't! That was just a safety precaution. After all, anyone could break into the surgery and then come up those stairs.'

'That door's never bolted when *you're* there, now is it?'

'I ought to keep it bolted I suppose – at night, at any rate. But I forget.'

'One evening he didn't even ask me in. We had to have our conversation on the doorstep,' Matty pursued relentlessly. 'In spite of a regular blizzard. That was the evening he was – entertaining.'

'Entertaining?'

'Well, I didn't see the people, but Mrs E. – she hadn't got an umbrella and decided to hang on until the weather had let up a little – well, she said that there was quite a party going on upstairs.'

'So you went up to investigate?' Lorna was suddenly rattled.

'I did no such thing. There were some things I had to ask him –
I'd lost your address for one thing and for another the gas-man
had tried to get in repeatedly to read the meter and was coming
back the next morning. No, I wasn't in the least interested in the
people he had up there. Why should I be?'

'But, Matty' – now Lorna was laughing and Matty began to
laugh with her – 'you *know* how inquisitive you are!'

'Well, perhaps I am, pet! But I saw no one because, as I say, I
was left to transact my business on the doorstep. All I heard was
this pop-music – and I'd been able to hear that downstairs too. A
ghastly row. Oh, and then this man – this tall man – appeared
from the kitchen and at once disappeared again. I just got a
glimpse, the merest glimpse, of him.'

'Perhaps that was Harry,' Lorna murmured, more to herself
than to Matty.

'Harry?'

'A friend of his – of ours,' she corrected herself. 'Harry Van
Fleet.'

'He'd visited Bob before. I'd seen him get into this huge
Mercedes one morning – oh, quite early. As I arrived for work.'

'He was here as early as that?'

'Well, he was probably dropping off a note or something on his
way to work,' Matty said, in a tone that made it clear that she
believed no such thing. She surveyed Lorna from under those
hooded lids to see the effect that this final revelation might have
had on her. But Lorna's face, shut and secret, betrayed nothing,
since she was determined that it should betray nothing.

'No, I don't think he had a dull time while you were away. Not
at all. In fact, I should say that he had rather a gay time, all in all.'
Again the eyes under the hooded lids surveyed Lorna, as some
tired eagle might survey its future prey. 'Well, you wouldn't want
him to brood in your absence, would you, pet? . . . Would you?'

Lorna shook her head.

'No, of course not.'

25

The next Sunday Bob seemed unusually restless, even jittery. Lorna heard him moving about only a few minutes after seven; and this was all the odder because he had returned so late the night before. The water gurgled and thumped through the antique plumbing not once but repeatedly. The stairs creaked as he went up and down them and finally she could hear the distant sound of his wireless, as he listened to yet another news bulletin. Normally they did not have breakfast until ten o'clock at the earliest, but unable to sleep any longer through all this activity, Lorna scrambled out of bed at barely eight.

'Lorna?'

She was passing his door on her way down to the bathroom.

'Yes. I'm up. What's the matter with you?'

'Nothing. Why?'

'You don't usually surface as early as this. Particularly when you've made a late night of Saturday. I thought perhaps you had an upset tummy or something of that kind.'

'No. I just couldn't sleep. I don't know why.'

He had always been one of those people who, when they cannot sleep themselves, unconsciously make it as difficult as possible for anyone else to do so.

In her dressing-gown – he was dressed – Lorna fried him their usual Sunday breakfast of bacon and eggs. But after a mouthful or two he pushed his plate aside and, surprisingly, took a packet of cigarettes from his pocket. She had never known him to smoke so early. She peered at the packet to see if it were one of Marlboros, but it was not.

'Don't you want to eat any more?'

'Somehow I don't seem to have any appetite. Don't know why. Sorry about the waste.'

'Anna will eat the bacon.'

'I wonder if that wretched boy has brought the papers yet.' He jumped up, for the second time, to see if they were lying on the mat. 'God, he's slack!' he exclaimed, returning. 'He gets later and later.'

'It's simply that we've got earlier – much earlier. You've never looked for them as early as this on a Sunday.'

As she dressed – by then she had had one of those 'urgent' calls from a patient that seldom proved to be really urgent – Bob shouted up to her:

'I'm slipping out for a moment.'

'Where are you going?'

'Oh, just for a spot of fresh air.'

'But it's raining!'

'Drizzling. That won't hurt me. I'll put on a mac.'

She went out of her room to tell him that she would soon be off to see her patient but, as she did so, she heard the front door slam behind him.

At lunch, too, he merely toyed with the roast lamb that she had put down before him.

'You're not well.'

'I'm perfectly all right!'

'It's not like you not to eat. You always have such a good appetite.'

'Oh, for Christ's sake, Lorna! Can't you leave me in peace!'

She compressed her lips, her body rigid as she leant forward to help herself to more of the mint sauce. 'I'm sorry.'

He reached for one of the Sunday supplements that he had thrown on to an empty chair and began to leaf through it, supporting it on a knee.

'You've finished?'

'I've finished.'

Suddenly she felt a rage well up within her. 'I must say this is one of the most amusing meals we've eaten together.'

'Do we *have* to talk all the time, all the time? Can't we just for a few minutes become unconscious of each other?'

'I daresay it could be managed.' She speared a slice of the

expensive leg of lamb off his plate with her fork. 'Come on, Anna! Anna!' The Siamese bounded forward.

In the sitting-room they sat in silence on either side of the gas fire, drinking their coffee. Though it was the blend she always bought and though she had made it in exactly the same way that she had always made it, it tasted unusually bitter and muddy on her tongue.

Bob jumped up and flicked the television from channel to channel, while she watched him in growing annoyance. Then the screen went blank. 'What rubbish!'

'No news bulletin for the moment.'

'There *are* other things I enjoy watching.'

'Are there?'

A moment later he had again jumped up, this time to go to the window to look out into the raw, rain-spattered March afternoon, his face discontented and forlorn as he held it near the pane, one hand on the curtain and the other pressed against his cheek.

'God, what weather!'

'It's the usual weather for this time of year.'

'And God what a country!' He turned, as though he had suddenly reached a decision while staring out at the cars glistening mistily through the gloom. 'I think I'm going away for a while. On a trip.'

'A trip! Where to?'

He shrugged. 'Take the motorbike. Spain perhaps. Maybe make my way over to Morocco. Find some sun. As you did in Agadir. I must have some sun. I can't stand this endless rain and mist and gloom, unutterable gloom.'

'What about your work?'

'What work? There isn't any. I've had precisely two days in the last two weeks.'

'Perhaps you should think of something else.'

'Perhaps I should. But first I want a change of scene.'

'Can you afford one?' she demanded implacably.

'Just. Yes. I have something put away.' Suddenly he turned on her. 'Do you *have* to pry?'

'Provided you don't expect me to stump up.'

'Is it likely?'

She nearly answered 'Very'. But she swallowed back the word, shrinking from a display of savagery as cruel as his own.

'Yes, I think I'll set off the day after tomorrow. That'll give me a day to get the bike into perfect order.'

'So soon!'

He nodded, suddenly relaxed after all the tension. He came and sat down, hands folded in his lap and legs out-stretched. He smiled at her: 'There's nothing to keep me. And every reason for getting going.'

'It seems rather – sudden. You've made no plans.'

'I don't need plans. I'll just set off and go where the spirit takes me. That's how I like to do things.'

She sipped at what was left of the bitter, lukewarm coffee in the bottom of her cup, making a slight grimace. Then she said: 'Yes, I can see that life must get rather boring for you here.'

He went on smiling, no longer at her but into the fire. He did not contradict her.

26

It was shortly after five o'clock in the morning. Anna was sleeping curled up in front of the paraffin stove in the hall, when Lorna made her way downstairs to prepare breakfast for Bob. He had been moving about the house for at least an hour before; now he was shaving.

Lorna yawned, not bothering to raise a hand to her mouth, and then shivered both from the chill of the kitchen and from disagreeable anticipation. There was something wrong with the fluorescent light overhead; there had been something wrong with it for several days. 'It only needs this slight adjustment,' Bob told her repeatedly. But still it flickered and now it would no doubt go on flickering until he came back or she called in an electrician to put it to rights.

'You shouldn't have got up,' he said. Smoothly shaved and with his hair plastered down – presumably he had had a bath – he stood in the kitchen doorway, hands deep in the pockets of the new anorak that she had given him as a farewell present.

'Oh, I couldn't sleep. And besides, I wanted to see you off.'

'It's not as though I were going away for ever. Is it?' He looked down at the anorak and then circled before her. 'Rather *chic*, don't you think?' Bright red, with two parallel lines of black running down each sleeve, and so padded that it made him look unnaturally burly, it was not the anorak that she herself would have chosen for him. But it was the one that he had insisted that he wanted.

'Very.'

'Thanks a lot for it again.' He came to her, put his arms round her and kissed her on the cheek, making her feel clumsy and vaguely embarrassed as she stood frozen with a slice of bread in her hand.

'I don't know why you have to set off at this unearthly hour,' she said, as she had said a number of times already. She dropped the slice of bread into the toaster. 'It's not as though you had to be at some particular place at some particular time.'

'Well, I might as well catch the first boat. Then I can get really moving across France before dark.'

'There you are!' She scooped up the egg that she had fried for him and placed it beside the bacon. 'You'd better make a good meal with that long run before you.'

'It's not all that far to Dover.'

She sat down opposite him, conscious of how slatternly she must look with no make-up on her face and in a dressing-gown that was blotched with stains and frayed under an armpit. She cupped her chin in her hands, her elbows on the table. 'At least you've got a good appetite this morning,' she commented, as he devoured the food before him.

He nodded. 'Yep.' Then he looked up. 'Aren't you going to eat anything?'

'Not now. Too early. I'll just have a cup of tea.' She reached for the teapot, the sleeve of the dressing-gown falling back to reveal her strong, capable arm. 'I wish I had an address for you.'

'I've already told you – I just don't know where I'll be going, let alone where I'll be staying. I don't want to tie myself down at all. That's the whole point of this trip. To be free, totally free.'

'There might be an emergency . . .'

'I doubt it. And if there is, you and Matty are perfectly capable of dealing with it. More efficiently than I could.'

'The emergency might involve us. One of us or perhaps even both of us.'

'That's a rather morbid thing to say.' He laughed. 'Anyway, sweetie, I'll be calling you frequently. These days long-distance calls are not all that expensive. And if the worst comes to worst, then I'll just reverse the charges.'

Lorna sighed. 'I'd still feel much happier . . .' She raised her cup in both hands and sipped at it.

'What a worrier you are! I'm only going away for ten days, two weeks, three weeks at the utmost.'

'Yes, I know. But – well, I'll miss you.'

'You've told Edie of my going?'

Lorna nodded. 'I rang her yesterday.'

'Well, then, you'll have her round. She might even come to stay. Who knows? If things continue to go badly with that boyfriend of hers.'

Lorna stood shivering outside the front door as Bob proceeded to load up the motorbicycle.

'Where did you get that rucksack?' she asked at one moment.

'This one?' he queried, although there was no other. 'Oh, I managed to borrow it.'

'Who from?' she would have liked to ask. Something told her that it had come from Harry Van Fleet. But instead she said fretfully: 'Do take care.'

'I always take care. Have you ever known me not to take care?'

'Often. And take particular care about your injections, won't you?' She had personally supervised the packing of adequate supplies of disposable syringes and insulin. 'You know how you have a way of forgetting them when you have other things on your mind.'

At last he was ready.

'Goodbye, old girl.' He put his arm around her and for the second time that morning his lips went to her cheek. 'How cold you are!' Her skin was icy and she had shivered involuntarily at the moment of contact.

'Well, it's not exactly the warmest day of the year.'

'Take care,' he called out, repeating her own advice to him, as he ran down the steps. He put on first his goggles and then his crash-helmet and finally adjusted his scarf so that it covered almost all the lower half of his face. All at once he became anyone and no one; and this anonymity, so casually assumed, filled her with a sudden, unreasoning panic. She had to hear him speak again, just to make sure that it was really he behind all these disguises.

'Yes?' His voice was muffled by the scarf; it seemed to come to her from far away, over the air or through a telephone cable.

'You will be careful? Promise!'

He nodded. She thought that he was smiling but she could not be sure because of that scarf. Then he kicked the huge machine into life, with a shattering noise that would no doubt have all the neighbours sleepily cursing as it roused them in their beds. A hand waved, the tyres screeched as he made a circle before her. Then he was gone.

She remained shivering, hands tucked under armpits, on the doorstep until the last faint reverberation of the powerful engine had faded on the icy air. Then she returned back into the house, where Anna lazily raised herself from the floor, stretched, yawned and finally deigned to take a series of dainty steps towards her.

Lorna picked up the cat and held it against her cheek. Its purr, drumming on endlessly, was like a diminished echo of the motorbicycle.

27

'What news of your brother?' It was the girl, an unmarried mother, who came in three times a week to cope with the clerical work of the practice for them. Competently brisk, she seldom showed any interest in the private lives of either of her employers and expected them to show none in hers.

'There hasn't been any. Ten days now – no, eleven – and not a word from him. It's rather worrying.'

'I don't call that long,' the girl said in the no-nonsense, slightly contemptuous tone that she tended to use to Lorna but, strangely, never to Matty. 'What's ten – or eleven – days, when one's on holiday?'

'It's not like him.'

'When one's travelling, one loses account of time. And in a country like Spain – or Morocco – it's not always easy to get through a long-distance call.'

Matty had dragged herself into the room, where the girl was seated at her typewriter with her child, a boy of three or four – Lorna could never remember his precise age – playing peacefully with a large rag doll around her feet. 'You're not still worrying about Bob?' she asked.

Lorna nodded.

'Well, that's silly.'

'That's just what I've been telling her,' the girl took up.

'You know what he's like', Matty said. 'He doesn't *think*. No news is good news – that's what he's telling himself. Just so as to save himself the expense and trouble of having to write or telephone.'

'He could send a card.'

'Perhaps he has.' The girl reached for yet another of her

Gauloise cigarettes; Matty hated their smell and often complained about it to Lorna and Mrs Emerson, but never to the girl herself. 'But you've no idea what posts are like in those countries. I had this boy-friend once in Italy. Half our letters never reached each other. And when they did, they were weeks and weeks late.' Lorna wondered if this boy-friend in Italy were the father of the child, who had lustrous, dark eyes and an olive complexion totally unlike his mother's.

'It's too silly to get yourself worked up this way,' Matty said in the cross, scolding tone that she always adopted when Lorna spoke of her anxieties for Bob. 'If anything had happened to him, you'd have heard. He's having a jolly good time, if you're asking me, and has forgotten all about Parson's Green and the practice and us.'

Lorna sighed. 'I hope you're right.'

Upstairs – she could hear the typewriter still clattering up from the basement – she stood before the paraffin stove, her hands outstretched so that her chilblains itched with its warmth, and wondered miserably. Probably Matty and the briskly, brusquely efficient girl were right: he had been too busy to write or telephone, or he had written and the letter or postcard had failed to get through, or he had not been able to place a long-distance call without an interminable wait for which – not surprisingly, given his nature – he had failed to find the patience. But was no news really good news? Her experience in life had taught her the opposite: no news was usually bad news. If something had happened to him – if he had had an accident or if he had run out of money or if he were in trouble – well, would she really have heard so quickly and certainly from some country like Morocco or Spain?

Staring at the flickering blue flame, while the typewriter clacked on below, she saw him first sprawled across a road with the motorbicycle crouched like some devouring monster above him; and then fever-ridden, incoherently gasping her name, as the flies buzzed round the ceiling of a narrow, high room of a native hotel in some casbah. Finally she saw – and the surprising, unsought vision filled her with a dread far chillier than any before it – a prison cell and his bruised, lacerated body sprawled in one corner as an officer stood, jackbooted feet wide apart, above him . . .

How had *that* vision come to her? She did not know. But her previous vague foreboding had now become acute.

28

Two days later Lorna and Matty were making a hurried lunch of bread and cheese and fruit. 'It's quite like the old days,' Matty had said, cutting herself a thick wedge of Cheddar. She meant that it was like the days before Bob had returned to disrupt the closeness of the relationship between the two of them. She munched contentedly, looking around her as she did so; and suddenly Lorna was reminded of an occasion when Anna had been mysteriously lost for several days, to return, emaciated and plaintive. In no time at all, she too had re-established herself in the household; and she too had looked around the kitchen with that same quiet, self-congratulatory satisfaction as she devoured the minced chicken set before her. 'But you're eating nothing, pet!'

'Oh, I never eat very much at midday.'

'You're all strung up, aren't you? I can see it a mile off. I've not known you all these years, come wet, come shine, for nothing. But it's so *silly* to get yourself into a tizz about him.'

'He's been gone thirteen days.' Suddenly Lorna thought: Unlucky thirteen! 'It's not like him not to write or telephone.'

Matty speared a gherkin from the pickle jar before her. 'Perhaps he felt the impulse to do something that was *un*like him. That's the most probable explanation.'

'What do you mean?'

'Well, pet, he may have suddenly wanted to make some kind of assertion of independence.'

'Independence!'

'He has been rather under your thumb ever since his return.'

'Not at all! He's been totally free. So free that I've rarely known *what* he's been doing. Or whom he's been seeing for the matter of that.'

'Still, you must admit . . .'

It was the old argument; Lorna was determined not to repeat it. Getting to her feet, she began brutally to clear the table even though Matty had far from finished.

'Have we time for a cup of coffee?' Matty asked.

Lorna looked at her watch. They had plenty of time but she answered: 'I'm afraid *I* haven't. But do make yourself some if you'd like to. I've got a huge number of calls. And one of them's to that Polish woman – you know the one I mean.'

'The one who took against me?'

'Did she? I don't remember.' In fact, Lorna remembered very well. Matty, whose political opinions were by most standards right-wing, had got into an acrimonious argument with the even more right-wing countess about the pre-war treatment of Jews in Poland. 'Anyway she always wastes my time.'

'You should be tougher with her.'

'I can't. Any more than I can be tough with poor Mrs Page. If they didn't talk to me, they'd have no one to talk to.'

'Mrs Page has that vegetable,' Matty said brutally. 'She can talk to it all day long and never get answered back.' It was unlike her to be so cruel and Lorna was shocked.

'Well, I'd better be off.'

'Perhaps I will make myself a cup of coffee.'

'Do!'

'Don't worry, pet. *Don't worry!* It's pointless. Utterly pointless.'

29

That evening, not waiting to eat first even though hunger had now started to gnaw at her entrails in the same way that anxiety had been doing, Lorna began to search through the telephone book. First she looked under the 'Fs' and then under the 'Vs'. There were a number of Van Fleets, three of them with the initial H, but only one of these last three had an address in Chiswick and she remembered that it was there that they had been returning on that night of the theatre. But having traced the likely number, she found herself terrified by the prospect of actually speaking to Van Fleet. She would need a drink first.

Eventually, having swallowed half a tumbler of neat gin in three or four gulps, she dialled the number, to be answered by a woman whom she assumed to be Mrs Van Fleet.

'He's not here, I'm afraid,' this woman said when Lorna asked for 'Mr Van Fleet'. 'He won't be back until tomorrow morning.'

'Tomorrow morning?' Lorna wondered if Mrs Van Fleet had guessed at her identity. The neat gin was burning away somewhere just below her diaphragm. 'Oh, he's away then?'

'Yes. He's away.' Mrs Van Fleet — yes, it was obviously her — sounded impatient to end the call.

'In Spain?' Suddenly Lorna had made a connection between the two absences, Bob's and Van Fleet's.

'In *Spain*! No. In the States. He's been there for two days on business . . . Who is it calling?'

So evidently Mrs Van Fleet had not recognized her.

Lorna hesitated for a moment and then said: 'Oh, I'm ringing for Dr Spencer.' Why Matty's name should have been the first to come into her mind she did not know.

'Dr Spencer?'

'Yes. He wanted a word with Mr Van Fleet. I'm his secretary.'

'Well, you'd better ring tomorrow. But you'd better ring the office. He'll probably go straight on there when his plane gets in. Sometime after midday you should catch him.'

'What is the office number?'

'Haven't you got it?'

'I *did* have it. But I seem to have mislaid it. And I don't seem to have any record of the name of his firm.'

'Metropolitan and Suburban.' She added a city number. Then she demanded, 'What does Dr Spencer want to talk to him about? If it's a business call surely you must –'

'Yes, it's a business call. Thank you so much. Sorry to have disturbed you. I'll ring the office.'

With thumping heart and a horrible feeling of rasping dryness in her mouth, Lorna carefully replaced the receiver on its cradle.

30

The next day Matty once more came upstairs for lunch. Lorna had not been able to avoid inviting her, since she had arrived at the surgery with the present of a large slice of Brie and a bag of pears. As before, Matty munched and gobbled greedily while Lorna barely ate a mouthful.

'You can't go on like this.'

'I know I can't. But what am I to do?' Lorna felt near to tears.

'Put him out of your mind.' Matty was brutally decisive.

'I *can't* put him out of my mind – any more than I could put you.'

Matty grunted.

At last the dreadful meal was over. This time, fortunately, it was Matty who had to hurry off. 'She's always ringing up about that daughter of hers. One would think she was a baby, not a grown woman. But if just for once one refused to go, you can be certain it would be the one occasion, out of all the hundreds and hundreds, when there was something really seriously amiss.'

'I'd go for you but I feel utterly done in.'

'Sweet of you, pet.' Matty put out a hand and patted Lorna's cheek. 'But this is my pigeon, not yours.'

As soon as Matty had dragged herself down the stairs into the basement, Lorna shut the dividing door and then, for no adequate reason, pushed across the bolt, before she went into the sitting-room to telephone.

'Metropolitan and Suburban,' a voice sang out.

'Mr Van Fleet, please.'

'Sorry?'

'Mr Van Fleet.'

'One moment, please. I'll try to connect you with his secretary.'

Next an obviously upper-class woman's voice – Lorna visualized a head of carefully set, close-cut grey hair, a twin-set and pearls – said, 'Mr Van Fleet's office.'

'Is Mr Van Fleet there?' She was conscious that the receiver had become slithery in the sweating palm that held it.

'Who is it please?'

'Dr Martin. Dr Lorna Martin.'

'I'll just see if he's in.'

It seemed improbable that his personal secretary did not know if he were in or not.

'I'm terribly sorry but he must have just slipped out for lunch. Can I take a message?'

'I must speak to him. Now. Would you please make sure that he isn't there. It's urgent. Very urgent.'

There was another silence, longer than the first, and then Lorna heard:

'Harry Van Fleet.'

'Oh, Mr Van Fleet, this is Lorna Martin.'

'Lorna Martin?' He sounded as if he genuinely did not know who she was.

'Bob's sister.'

'Bob? Are you sure you've got the right number?'

'Yes. We met at the theatre. Don't you remember? And then we talked that time when you were waiting by Parson's Green. You must know who he is – and who I am. You even visited our house when I was away in Morocco.'

'Oh, of course. *Of course!* How silly of me. I've just got back from New York and I'm still in a daze. Jet-lag. Do please forgive me. What can I do for you?'

'It's about my brother. About Bob.'

'Yes?' Did she imagine it or was there something guarded, even frightened behind the bonhomie. 'What's the trouble exactly?'

'He's – well, he's vanished.'

'Vanished? How do you mean?'

Hurriedly, stumbling over words and correcting and recorrecting herself, she tried to explain; and meanwhile at the other end of the line he made an occasional sympathetic or puzzled interjection.

At the end he said: 'But why do you think *I'd* know where he is?'

'Well – seeing as how you're – you're friends ... I mean, he might just have told you something – or written to you ...'

There was a strange, prolonged silence, in which she wondered if he had put down the telephone. Then he said: 'No, he told me nothing and he certainly hasn't written to me. I don't know your brother all that well, you know.'

'Yes, perhaps I shouldn't have bothered you. I'm sorry. But as you'd visited the house ...'

'Well, I did call there once. Bob probably told you that he did one or two little jobs for the firm.'

'Jobs?'

'Didn't he tell you that?'

'I'd no idea. No.'

'How extraordinary!'

'He's very secretive.'

'Well, that's no bad thing. Not that there was – is – anything secret about the jobs ... Yes, he used to guide some of our foreign visitors for us. Mostly people from the part of the world he knows. Singapore, Kuala Lumpur. One or two from Japan. Hong Kong. So when I called at the house, it was simply to tell him about this Chinese businessman – an important contact ...'

Lorna knew that he was lying. Unless, of course, Matty had been lying. But what reason would Matty have had to tell her lies?

'And you've no idea where he might be now?'

'None at all.'

'Did he tell you he was going abroad?'

'I believe he said something about it. Yes, he must have done. Because we had this visitor from K.L. only two days ago and in the ordinary course of things ...'

A sense of overwhelming impotence descended on her.

'Well, thank you,' she said. 'I'm sorry to have taken up your time.'

'Anything to be of service.'

It sounded faintly ironic.

31

If you can't get to sleep, that usually means that you're suffering from anxiety. But if you wake up too early in the morning, that's usually a symptom of depression. She had said that often enough to her patients and they had seemed to believe her; and yet here she was, awake at half past four in the morning, after at once falling into a deep sleep as soon as she had gone to bed, and surely it was anxiety, not depression, that was racking her?

Lying on her back, with her hands behind her head, while Anna's purr throbbed on and on beside her as though it were some outer manifestation of this blind abscess that throbbed on and on within, she went over the telephone conversation with Harry Van Fleet, over and over, seeking for some nuance or unintended hint that might, until then, have eluded her. Yes, he had been disconcerted by her call, he had even been frightened; and yes, he had been lying to her – he knew Bob far better than he had wished to admit to her and he had certainly visited the house more than once in her absence.

Probably – no, certainly – there had been some kind of sexual relationship between the two of them. Bleakly now she accepted as fact what, until then, she had refused to admit to be more than a supposition. Such a relationship – and perhaps others like them – would explain Bob's evasions and lies about his movements and contacts; and it would also explain Harry Van Fleet's reluctance to admit that he knew Bob as anything other than someone who, from time to time, did a job for the firm.

But that did not throw any light on the twin mysteries of Bob's abrupt departure and of his subsequent silence. Unless of course – she felt as though a sudden blow had been struck upwards within her – Bob, chronically short of money, had attempted to blackmail Harry Van Fleet and Van Fleet had then arranged for his convenient disappearance ... Oh, but that was too absurdly melo-dramatic! And yet Bob was the sort of person of whom no one, not even she, could say with total confidence 'But he'd never attempt such a thing'; and Harry – a tough, self-made man, eager to preserve his marriage to the woman from whom his money had derived – well, did she know him well enough to say that *he* would never attempt such a thing? No, of course she didn't. Perhaps ... yes, perhaps on that evening when, so bafflingly, he had said that he was meeting someone by Parson's Green, he had really been watching Bob, spying on him; or perhaps genuinely there had been someone else and that someone else was the henchman whose task it was to be to see that Bob was silenced either temporarily or – who knows? – for ever. At best, Bob might have been given some sum of money and told to vanish; at worst the vanishing might have been an actual physical erasure ...

Oh, but this was the sickest of fantasies! It was on a par with what that advertising executive's wife used to tell her about her suspicions that her husband was trying to poison her and her children; and she, poor woman, was now in the Maudsley and the husband had got a divorce from her (so, finally, he had in a sense got rid of her) and had married again. She now had no more evidence than that deluded woman had produced first in the consulting-room and then to the police. It was all some kind of paranoic waking nightmare from which she must somehow rouse herself if she were to recover her sanity. And yet ...

She threw back the bedclothes, got out of bed, slipped into her dressing-gown. Then, feet bare, she walked out of her bedroom and into Bob's. She stood there in the semi-darkness – the curtains were undrawn – and looked frantically around her, as though somewhere, on the bed or in the chairs or in the shadows cast by the trees on the wall beside her, she would find the certainty of either a confirmation or a denial of her deepest fears. But there was no such certainty, none, none.

She turned slowly round and round, round and round, in the dark, empty, icy room. Then all at once, hands pressed to her lips, she burst into choking sobs.

32

The offices were emptying. Lorna watched the girls scurrying out in groups of two and three; an elderly woman – could this be the secretary to whom she had spoken? – carefully negotiating the steps that led down from the pompous late-Victorian portico, one hand to the highly polished railing while the other clutched a bag the size of a satchel; two languid young men in high collars, one of whom brandished an unfurled umbrella for emphasis as they talked animatedly for a period before they went their separate ways; men older, more decorous and obviously more important. The car felt airless even though the window beside her was wound down to its full extent and a wind was shaking the row of leafless saplings planted the length of the curving street. She unbuttoned her coat and eased away the collar. Perhaps he had left by some other exit; perhaps he had left before her arrival; perhaps he was already on some other plane to some other remote destination, where he was making yet more money.

She had set out on an impulse, as soon as the last of her afternoon calls was over. She had told Matty that she might be late for surgery, without giving her any reason other than 'It looks as if this one is going to take some time'. Matty had called out after her 'Who is it?' but she had pretended not to hear as she had run up the outside steps. There would be grumbling in the waiting-room and the other receptionist, who doubled with Mrs Emerson, would adopt her usual bossy manner to quell it and then herself grumble that once again she had been made late in getting home. Probably, almost certainly the impulse had been folly; but she had to know more than she had learned from that inconclusive telephone call and she felt that only by actually confronting Van Fleet could she know that more.

An elderly Austin Princess, driven by a chauffeur, drew up

outside the building; it was not Van Fleet, however, but a white-haired, white-moustached man who got into it. Some more girls clattered down the steps, their laughter shrilly grating.

Then, all at once, there he was, hatless and with a briefcase in one hand, with a younger man, his hair to his narrow shoulders, beside him. The young man, nervously gauche, swung his whole body back and forth as they exchanged a few words; then Van Fleet gave a brusque nod of the head, the young man sketched a gesture that was half-way between a deferential salute and a wave and they separated. As they did so the Rover that had been waiting beyond Lorna moved gently forward; and at that, having clambered out of her own car, she dashed across the street. She had been expecting the Mercedes.

'Mr Van Fleet!'

He looked at her as he had spoken to her on the telephone: as though she were a stranger.

'Yes?'

'You remember me, don't you? Lorna Martin. Bob's sister.'

'Oh, yes.' The tone was icily distant and distancing.

'I wanted to have a word with you. Could you spare me a moment?'

Van Fleet looked over to the Rover – the military-looking chauffeur, whom she remembered from that evening at the theatre, was now standing beside it, a gloved hand on the handle of the door – and then at her and then back to the car again, while his mouth pursed in exasperation.

'I'm in an awful hurry.'

'Please! Just a minute. I won't keep you long.'

'This is not exactly the best place for a conversation.'

'We could talk in my car.' She pointed.

He hesitated a moment; then he shrugged. 'I'll be with you in a second, Smiley,' he called across to the chauffeur.

'Thank you. I know I'm being an awful nuisance but I've been so – so desperately worried . . .'

As he settled himself beside her in the car, he drew in his breath sharply and said: 'I don't honestly see how I can help you any further.'

'I have a feeling – a hunch – that you may know Bob better than you want me to think.'

'I don't know where you've got that idea from.' He spoke in an off-hand, almost bored tone; but she was certain that she had succeeded in rattling him with her directness, as she had planned to do. 'I know him about as well as I know a lot of the people who do occasional jobs for us.'

'I think you've seen him often these last months.'

He laughed. 'I can assure you I haven't. I don't know what he may have told you but really –'

'Bob tells me nothing. But I – I *know*.'

Under that orange tan – acquired, she suspected, from an ultra-violet lamp – he seemed to have paled. 'And how do you know?' Again his tone was deliberately off-hand, almost bored.

'Bob and I are very close,' she said slowly. 'We always have been. We don't have to tell things to each other. There's this – this silent kind of communication between us.'

'Some sort of ESP?' He gave a short laugh.

'I think you know where he is. Or, at least, why he went away.'

He swivelled round in his seat now and smiled into her face. The smile was not a pleasant one, the mouth a gash in the long, narrow face and the eyes chilly in their arctic blueness. 'I simply can't account for such an extraordinary delusion. Your brother has certainly never made a confidant of me, I can assure you. Doesn't this ESP extend to your divining his whereabouts?'

'Please tell me the truth! I know you're not telling me the truth.'

He reached for the door-handle beside him. 'Look, I'm in an awful hurry. I've got an appointment at six and I'm going to be late for it.'

'You visited the house a number of times while I was away.'

He let go of the handle; his body became suddenly still and stiff. 'You've been misinformed,' he said curtly.

'I don't think so.'

He thought a moment, the fingers that had held the handle now moving to his lips. Then he said: 'Well, perhaps I do know your brother a little better than I've let on. Or *did* know him. Because some time ago I decided that it perhaps was better – wiser – not to go on knowing him.'

'What do you mean?'

'Well, there were certain features of his life-style that seemed to me – that did not quite fit in with my own style of life.'

'Such as?'

'I'd prefer not to be too explicit. Since you know so much about your brother, you must know about them too.'

Lorna hesitated for a moment. Then she said: 'Of course I've – I've *guessed* at certain things . . .'

'Well then!'

'But I just don't understand – can't begin to guess – why he should have disappeared in this extraordinary fashion.'

'If you're so worried, oughtn't you to consult the police? Or perhaps you've done that already?' But he knew, of course, that she hadn't.

'I'd rather not do that. Not for the moment . . . Do you think – please be frank with me, Mr Van Fleet – do you think that, well, there might have been any *reason* for his wanting – or having – to disappear?'

He shrugged. 'I've no idea. No idea at all.' And again she knew that he was lying. He had some knowledge that she did not have.

'You were talking about his – his *life-style*. What exactly did you mean by that?'

'Well, I don't want to spell it all out. But his conduct could be – let's face it – rather unconventional. And perhaps – well, it's just conceivable . . .' He broke off.

'Yes?'

'He may have gone too far.'

'Too far?' Once again she felt that terror and despair of the early hours, with the cat throbbing beside her and that blind abscess throbbing away within. 'How do you mean?'

He shrugged. 'Perhaps he was – how shall we say? – a little imprudent.' Suddenly and mysteriously his accent seemed to have become more exaggeratedly Australian. Again his hand went to the door-handle. 'And now really . . .' He opened the door, put out a long leg.

'Oh, just one moment more! Please!'

He shook his head over the shoulder of his beautiful Crombie coat. 'Sorry. Can't be done. Look!' He held out the flat gold disc of his watch to her, the orange hairs of his wrist glistening in the light that had come on behind him with the opening of the door. 'Past six. I must get to that appointment.'

'Some other time,' she pleaded. 'Any time.'

'But – Lorna' – he hesitated, as though ransacking his memory for a name of no importance – 'I've told you all I know. *All*. I wish I knew where your brother was. I wish I knew why he had vanished – if he *has* vanished. But I just don't. I honestly don't.'

He clambered out of the car and then leant in to it to say his final words. 'I liked your brother, you know, when first we met. He has great charm. He's – he's *fun*. But then slowly it was borne in on me that he was – well, he was just not for me. I can't put it more plainly than that. I'm sorry. Just not for me.'

Lorna extended a hand as though to clutch his sleeve and drag him towards her. But he took a step backwards, his crocodile-leather briefcase under one arm and that narrow gash of a smile cutting his face in two.

'I hope you have good news of him. Soon. I wish I could have been of greater help.'

Lorna said nothing, gazing ahead of her, her hands on the wheel.

'Goodbye – er – Lorna – Dr Martin.' Again he hesitated over her name. 'It was nice to see you.'

He gave an ironic little salute, raising a gloved hand to touch the brim of an invisible hat and bowing simultaneously. Then he was hurrying away from her towards the car that awaited to carry him to that long delayed appointment.

33

'I agree it's odd. But I don't really think you should at once assume the worst. I remember how I once got myself into a terrible state because I'd heard nothing for days and days from Donald that time he went to Crete. And then it turned out that he'd been writing to me almost daily but giving the letters to some boy at the hotel to post.'

Usually it was Edie who was distracted, depressed or distressed and Lorna who consoled and calmed. Now those roles had been reversed as they talked over dinner in the vast restaurant, refurbished in Art Deco style, at the top of the Kensington store. It was Edie who had first said, 'I'm going to take you out to cheer you up!' and had then chosen this place which to Lorna, who could remember shopping in the same building with her mother, carried too heavy a burden of childhood nostalgia to be cheerful.

'Yes, you may be right.' Lorna looked up at the rainbow of lights that circled the ceiling above them and wondered if she only imagined it or if it really swelled and contracted, swelled and contracted. 'But I just have this hunch.'

'Oh, you and your hunches! Do you remember when you had that hunch that Donald and I shouldn't fly on that plane to Jersey. And nothing happened, nothing at all! Except that we quarrelled all the time.'

Suddenly, as those coloured bars of light vibrated sickeningly above, Lorna felt the impulse to empty out all the anxieties within her. She had not been wholly truthful to Matty or Miranda; she had not yet been wholly truthful to this daughter of hers, once so close and now moving inexorably away from her into her own untidy but seemingly happy life of intermittent jobs, nomadic migrations from one shared flat or room to another and a whole series of relationships which seemed to fill her successively with delight, depression, despair and then, finally and most potently of all, an overmastering boredom.

'I've often wondered about Bob . . . I mean, he's never married, he's never been engaged. There used to be those girl-friends of course – when he was still at Oxford and just after. But I never felt them to be really serious. He *may* have women friends now – I can't say for sure that he doesn't, because he has this extraordinary secrecy thing. But somehow . . .' Her voice trailed away in embarrassment.

Edie looked at her closely, blowing out smoke through her nostrils. 'What *are* you trying to say, Mummy?'

'Well, there's this man.' That need to empty out everything within her overcame the embarrassment. 'He's – he's an Australian. Rich. Some kind of property speculator. Married. And I just sense this extraordinary kind of closeness between him and Bob. Something odd, a little frightening, sinister.' She went on to speak about Van Fleet's peremptory telephone calls; about seeing him that winter's evening in the failing light by Parson's Green; about his obvious discomfiture when she first rang him up and his even greater discomfiture when she actually confronted him; about his pretence that he had known Bob far less well than in truth. 'He must have come frequently to the house while I was away in Agadir – if Matty is to be believed. And she'd hardly *invent* something of that kind. Why should she?'

'Are you trying to suggest that Bob is queer or something?'

Lorna nodded. 'I think I've always known it. But as with so many things that one prefers not to know, I've put the knowledge away from me all these years. It's like one of my patients – a man who insisted that he wanted to know the prognosis for his illness. So I told him that, short of a miracle, I doubted if he would last more than a year. He was horrified, poor creature. But the next time I saw him – well, he'd just *forgotten*, it was as if that agonizing talk between us had never taken place!'

'I don't think you're right,' Edie said with disconcerting certainty. 'In fact, I'm bloody sure you're not. I can see that you might easily jump to that conclusion because, well, let's face it, Bob *is* queer, damned queer. But not queer in the way that is usually now meant by that word. Perhaps it would be better if he were.'

'What do you mean?'

'Well, if he were having it off with some rich Australian, it wouldn't really matter all that much, would it? Not nowadays. But his tastes are unfortunately rather more peculiar than that.'

Lorna stared across the table at her daughter in pathetic bewilderment. Edie shifted in her chair and reached for another cigarette to light from the one that was little more than a pinched fragment of paper and tobacco between her finger and thumb. 'I've never told you this before, because, well, there seemed no reason to tell you. Perhaps I shouldn't tell you now. It's bound to distress you. But I don't want you to feel distressed – or guilty – because you didn't see it all and didn't prevent its happening.'

Lorna still stared with blind, bewildered eyes at her daughter, the cigarette-smoke being blown across the table all at once filling her with nausea. 'I don't know what you're trying to say, darling. I just don't follow.'

'Bob likes little girls,' Edie said brutally. 'The littler, the better.'

Lorna gasped, a hand covering her mouth. 'Oh, no, darling! No!'

Edie nodded. 'Oh, yes, Mummy. Yes.'

'But he's never shown the least sign –'

'I happen to know. *I know*.' Edie blew out the smoke once again between her rounded lips; and suddenly Lorna realized the full horror of what she was trying to tell her.

'You mean that he . . .?'

Edie again nodded, wholly calm. 'Yes. And I let him. I was, oh, just eleven. And it went on for, yes, about ten months. Then I suddenly realized how nasty it all was and I – I told him so. And then it ended. He was very frightened,' she added, with grim pleasure. 'Scared stiff. When I ended it, I mean. He probably thought I'd run to you with the whole beastly story. But I didn't.'

'Oh, Edie! Edie! I wish that you had!'

'No.' Edie smiled, superior at last to her mother in assurance and wisdom. 'You'd have made a great thing of it. And the point was that it was honestly not all that important.'

'But how could it *not* be important?' Lorna cried out in anguish. She saw now why Edie came less and less to the house; why she had rejected any suggestion that she might take over the top storey as her flat; why she never wished to hear what Bob was doing or to talk to him or even to run into him on her visits.

Edie shrugged. 'Yes, I know that that kind of experience ought to have given me some hideous trauma – warped me for years if not for life. But, well, all I can say is that it didn't. Not at all. I daresay I seem a pretty odd fish to *you* but to most of my friends – well, I think they think me wholly normal. I have no hang-ups about sex, I can relate to others – men *and* women – with no difficulty at all. It shouldn't be like that, I know – not if the Freudians are right. But there it is.'

Lorna pressed her clasped hands against her mouth. 'I should have realized, I should have realized!'

'Oh, for God's sake, don't feel *guilty* about it. That's precisely why I've never told you the whole squalid story. It wasn't a *nice* thing to happen, I wish that it hadn't. But it means no more in my life now than that perforated appendix or the time when I was caught pinching that purse from Woolworths one half-term. As a matter of fact' – she laughed – 'something totally trivial rankles with me far more now – yes, still rankles with me – than anything that Bob ever did on all those occasions when he used to promise to keep an eye on me while you and Daddy went out.'

'Something trivial?' Lorna spoke like someone in deep shock, her voice tremulous and faint.

Again Edie gave her jolly, loud laugh. 'Do you remember how in the old days – in the dear dead days beyond recall two people could travel in a taxi without any extra charge? The extra charge only came with the third. Well, when you and Bob and I travelled in a taxi together, one or other of you would always say "That's five bob" – or whatever it was – "and there's an extra sixpence for Edie." It made me so angry, so sick – it still does – that *I* had to be the extra, always, always! Never you, never Bob!'

'But that's so silly!'

'Yes, I know it's silly, of course it's silly. But I can only say that something so silly sticks with me far more than those ten months of being groped and pawed by my beloved uncle.'

Lorna thought for a long time, staring across and up at those bands of colour that seemed to swell and contract, swell and contract before her aching eyes. She was passing through a period of terrible reappraisal. At last she said: 'This relationship with this Australian . . .?'

Edie shrugged. 'I don't know. Not having met him. But I don't believe for a moment that there's anything in the least bit homo about it. It's far more likely – if the Australian is, as you say, rich – that Bob procures for him.'

'*Procures*?'

'I'm only suggesting a possibility. Perhaps he, too – the Australian – has a taste for little girls. And perhaps Bob is cleverer – or bolder – at finding them than he is.'

'I've never really been able to understand how Bob manages to survive on what he earns from filming,' Lorna said in a slow, slurred voice. 'That was something else that I preferred not to think about.'

'Well, then!'

'You don't think . . .?' Suddenly the slow, slurred voice rose in pitch; then it sank.

'Yes?'

'Well, you don't think he *had* to leave the country? I mean, he might have – have done something silly.'

'It's a possibility. A distinct possibility.' Edie seemed almost pleased at being in a position to inflict these successive shocks on a mother whom she none the less loved, just as Matty had seemed actually to enjoy hurting this dearest of all her friends and having her at her mercy. 'I just don't know. No one's been to see you, have they?'

'Who do you mean?'

'Well, the police.'

'Of course not! No!'

Edie put out a hand, the forefinger orange with nicotine, and placed it over her mother's. 'It's no use worrying,' she said. 'Perhaps he thought it wiser to disappear for a little. And perhaps it really was. But sooner or later he'll come back again. And then, as like as not, you'll be able to forget the whole business.'

'Forget the whole business! But how could I? How *could* I?' She was no longer like that patient of hers, planning for a future into which it was impossible that he would survive. Here was something that she could not bury out of consciousness.

'Try,' Edie said. 'He means a lot to you. I know that.' She nodded with a certain bitterness, her mouth slightly twisted. 'The two of you probably mean more to each other than to anyone else. You had Daddy. Bob had me and no doubt goes on having other little girls. But basically for the two of you – well, you're a *pair*.'

This was, strangely, the deepest and the most agonizing of all the thrusts of the dagger.

34

She was inexplicably afraid now to enter that room. But she would have to do it, she knew that she would have to do it. She lay on her bed, fully clothed but for her shoes which she had kicked off untidily and, one hand to forehead, thought of all that Edie had told her. 'You're a *pair*!' Well, it was true enough. All their life they had been a pair, in a way that she and Alfred or she and Edie or she and Matty had never been. She had been a mother to him when his real mother had been far too taken up with her unremitting committees and voluntary work in the canteen of the Hammersmith Hospital and the WVS to act as one; and she had been a father to him, too, when Dada had superciliously shrugged off that role and made no secret of his dislike and contempt and then, finally, his loathing of this stepson of his. But there had been more than that and she struggled, the sweat cold and clammy on her forehead beneath the hand she had thrown across it, to identify what it was. The needle, she thought, the needle ... And she remembered those secret sessions when, tiptoeing so that Dada would not hear, she had gone into his room to give him the injection that he shrank in mingled terror and revulsion from giving to himself; those occasions when Dada either overheard or somehow divined what she was doing and would burst in on the room to upbraid them, as though they were engaged in something dishonest or immoral; the times, even now, when he would call out to her, to tell her that he just couldn't face it, that she must do it for him, that to plunge the needle into his own flesh was something too revolting for him to contemplate.

... And there had been her own secret pleasure, even joy in this dependence that the needle imposed on him. More than anything else – more than their alliance against Dada, their isolation in that house in which everyone else was too busy to pay them much attention, more than his economic reliance on her after he had returned from the Far East, incapable or unwilling to take up any regular job – it was that complicity, barely acknowledged between them, of injector and injected, the one who gave life and the one who received it, that bound them so close. In her mind she saw a whole succession of syringes: the old-fashioned ones, with the needles that became progressively blunter and blunter and had to be sterilized with so much care; and then the modern ones, as disposable as paper-tissues. She saw the flesh shuddering and shrinking not from the cold but from the anticipation of the moment when the metal plunged into it; she saw the wrinkled skin of the scrotum between the parted legs; she heard the sharp intake of breath, which was sometimes even followed by an involuntary whimper; she felt the cotton-wool in her fingers and smelled the alcohol. It was as though she were reliving the whole sequence of her marriage-night with Alfred; but whereas all those details – of Alfred's clumsy, middle-aged ardour and her own youthful fear and the embarrassment of them both, even shame – were now totally neutral in her mind (she might have been recollecting some long-ago operation in which she had taken part as an intern), the details of the needle brought her an intense, partly pleasurable and partly disagreeable excitement.

Then it was of Edie whom she thought. How could she have kept that secret, how could she! And it was no longer pity and disgust as in the restaurant but rage that now made her hand tremble on her sweating forehead; and the rage was not against him but against her, her daughter. She must have enjoyed it to let it go on like that month after month and then, at the end, to have breathed not a word. Of course she must. But how could the two of them have conspired together to deceive her in that way and how could she herself have been so stupid as not to guess at the deception? 'Bob and Edie are the most wonderful friends,' she would boast. Yes – only now the forgotten memory surfaced, like some monster from the dark, chill depths of the ocean floor – she had even referred to Bob as 'your best boy' or 'your chum' when talking of him to Edie. And Edie used then to give that funny, proud little smile of hers: the same smile that she now gave when

159

she produced the latest young man with whom she was sharing her disordered, nomadic life. Yet Edie was right: somehow that whole ghastly experience had left her untouched; she was, as she had claimed, wholly *normal*. It was she, Lorna, who would never be the same; it was she whom the abnormality of this brother had incurably infected.

She got off the bed and then sat on it, head in hands, while the cat, forgotten and unfed, circled her with a piteous mewing. 'Oh, get away!' She kicked out at it and kicked out again; and, astonished, the cat leapt away on to the dressing-table, where, silent, it began delicately to lick one paw, as though in civilized reproach for such an uncharacteristic act of barbarism. Every muscle aching, Lorna got up and, barefoot, went out into the passage. She put a hand out to the door-handle, barely daring to touch it as though its metal might be molten; then, steeling herself, she gave it a quick turn.

Unaired and untenanted for so long, the room had a curious smell, as of dead leaves in some corner of a winter garden. She went across and jerked the curtains together and only then put on the light, fumbling for the switch in a darkness that now pressed thick and hairy against her. The brightness, slashing down across her eyes, made her cringe. She opened a drawer and closed it on a jumble of socks and handkerchiefs; opened another drawer and closed that one on a jumble of shirts and pyjamas. It was not really in either of those that she was planning to look; the examination of them was in the nature of the limbering-up of an athlete faced with a challenge to which he fears that he is not equal. Finally she stooped and from beneath the high brass bedstead she drew out, breathing effortfully, the ancient tuck-box.

But of course she had forgotten her keys! She returned to her own bedroom – Anna squinted at her reproachfully, still on the dressing-table – and found the ring in a drawer of her desk. Many of the keys on it were rusty; many of them belonged to suitcases long since thrown away or to doors which she had not entered for years. One of them would surely fit.

The dust was thick on the lid of the tuck-box; soon her hands, leaving their marks, were grey with it. But though she struggled

160

with key after key, now gently easing and now thrusting and pushing, the lock resisted all of them. On that previous occasion it had all been so easy, with the second or third key turning without effort. Why should it now be so hard?

In a sudden frenzy of exasperation she raced down the stairs and pulled open the door to the little garden-room, unheated and therefore icy, in which they untidily stacked away anything – broken chairs, cabin-trunks, antiquated paraffin stoves and electric fires, skis, walking-sticks, dilapidated umbrellas – for which they no longer had a use but which they could not bring themselves to jettison. Here too was the tool-box, with its disorder of nails and screws and picture-wire entangled around hammers and pliers. She found a chisel, feeling the sharpness of it along her thumb, and then remounted the stairs to the bedroom, conscious, as never before, of how they creaked at each step.

Savagely she prised at the lock, chipping and denting the wood around it; and reluctantly it at last yielded with a screech – it might have been some living thing – to her onslaught. She raised the lid and looked down, as once before so many years ago, with a curious mingling of excitement and shock.

The first thing she saw was the cross, glinting up at her on its fine, broken chain. It was obviously cheap, probably not gold, possibly pinchbeck. She took it up in her hand, as though it were something somehow defiled and defiling, and then on an impulse pressed it to her lips, one of its arms sharp against them. There was a bangle, its thin gold circle adjustable, with a turquoise set in it. There was a small, shrivelled cardigan, baby blue in colour, with a Marks & Spencer's label. Underneath were three small transparent envelopes of the kind that Bob had used as a boy when he still collected stamps; perhaps these envelopes had come from that old store. Each contained a lock of hair: one oddly speckled as though woven from sand; one a springy, shiny black; one so fair that it seemed almost transparent as she held it, wondering, to the light. Then there were the newspaper cuttings, many of them yellowing: an old *Time Magazine* photograph of Shirley Temple and another of Petula Clark, the first titled 'Winsome Moppet'; photographs without any indication of whom they represented; one, blurred and grey, of a child with the information below it that she was missing and that her disappearance was causing grave concern to the police. At this last Lorna stared in horrified fascination, tilting it to the light. Surely Bob could not have been in any way concerned with that 'disappearance'?

Then, previously distraught and appalled, she suddenly felt an extraordinary resolution fill her. It was akin to the moment when, only twenty-three, she had with total calmness made an incision into the chest of a seemingly dying patient and massaged his heart, while a young Irish nurse had looked on with ashen face. She got off her knees, walked down to the kitchen and fetched a carrier bag. Into it she began to stuff the contents of the tuck-box. Then she went out into the garden, blundering across the lawn, now no more than a vague blur under the even vaguer blur of the misty sky, and fumbled to find a stone large enough and heavy enough for her purpose. She carried it upstairs, noticing fastidiously, as she mounted, that there was mud on the hem of her dress and on one of her stockings. She wrapped the stone in the shrivelled cardigan and then tied up this parcel with the scarlet hair-ribbon that only now she noticed coiled up neatly in one corner of the box. Was that everything?

The tuck-box had a smaller box on a hinge attached to it on one side and she suddenly realized, I haven't looked in that. She lifted the lid and saw a pair of knickers inside with a rusty stain along them. She shuddered as she touched them and then that extraordinary resolution filled her once again. She pushed them deep into the carrier bag. On top of everything she carefully folded an outdated copy of *The Times* that she found lying on Bob's desk.

Back in her own room she put on her shoes again and then descended the stairs, the carrier bag heavy on her arm and on her spirit. Anna leapt down behind her, mewing once again to be fed. 'Not now,' she told the cat. 'Later. Wait.' She slipped into her coat, retrieving it from where she had flung it down across the sofa in the sitting-room. It was a few minutes past eleven.

How much colder it seemed now than when, less than an hour before, she had kissed Edie goodbye outside the restaurant. 'Shall I see you home?' Edie had asked, obviously reluctant and yet feeling it to be her duty, and Lorna had answered, 'Oh, good heavens, no!'

Edie had been relieved, no doubt because she had arranged to meet Donald somewhere before the pubs had closed. 'Are you sure?'

'Quite sure. Parson's Green's so out of your way. And you know what public transport's like at this hour.'

'Perhaps I shouldn't have told you all that.'

'I'm glad you did.'

'You'd got it all so wrong.'

'Yes. So wrong.'

Lorna began to walk down a dark road, a funnel for the piercing wind that blew off the river that was now her destination. The bag swung back and forth from her arm as she strode unflinching onwards. She met hardly a soul: a drunk staggering and muttering; an elderly woman with an elderly spaniel, a bell tinkling from its collar; two youths and a girl, their arms interlinked. Then all at once a voice was calling to her: 'Oh, Dr Martin! Dr Martin!'

In the shadows of the steps of one of the huge semi-detached Victorian houses, its drive pocked with grass, someone was standing with something – a sack? – beside her. She knew that voice, of course, she knew it. But she did not wish to stop. 'Dr Martin!'

'Yes? ... Oh, it's you, Mrs Page. I couldn't see you in the darkness.'

Mrs Page came towards her along the weed-pocked drive, half-carrying and half-dragging a bag of shiny grey film crammed with refuse. For a crazy moment Lorna thought 'That's our bag! That's the one in which Bob left that blood-stained shirt!' But Mrs Page said 'I forgot to put this out. The men come so early. Everything's gone out of my head since – since ...' She gulped and then there was a sudden glistening in one corner of her eye, as she stooped and gave the bag another ferocious jerk. 'Unless it's by the gate, they just won't be bothered.' She propped the bag against a cast-iron bin, presumably the property of another of the tenants, and wiped her thin hands down her apron. Then she said, 'Dr Spencer told you, didn't she?'

'Told me?' The bag in Lorna's hand seemed terribly heavy now; she was sure that it was far heavier than that bag of refuse.

'About – about *him*.'

Lorna shook her head.

'But I told her to tell you!' the keeper of the grub wailed out in a mingling of anguish and exasperation. 'How could she have forgotten? She promised me, she promised! Of course I wanted you to know, I knew that you would want to know. You were so kind to him. Perhaps if it hadn't been her but you ... But she explained that it was her night on duty.'

'I don't understand.' Lorna shook her head as though to shake away something invisible yet suffocating that was closing around it.

'He passed away. Late last night – just after four o'clock – he passed away. I'm sure if you'd been able to come ...'

'Oh, I'm sorry. I'm sorry.' But she could hardly take it in, the string of the bag cutting into her palm and that piercing wind funnelling up the narrow, winding street from the river to which she must go on her appalling errand.

'You understood his illness.' Now Mrs Page sounded aggressive, even accusing. 'You knew how to deal with him. She never did, never! You were the one.'

'But, Mrs Page ...' She felt a terrible weariness but somehow she forced herself to continue. 'Don't you understand? It was a miracle – yes, really, a miracle – that he managed to last all those years. Four, was it? Five? He could have gone any time during all that period. If he'd gone into an institution, well, he'd have been dead long ago. It was only because of your devotion ...'

Suddenly, at that mention of the devotion expended on tending the grub, the other woman began to sob with wild, incoherent gulps, as though an invisible hand were tightening about her throat and she were fighting for air.

'Mrs Page! Don't do that! You did all that was possible for him.' Lorna put an arm round her shoulder, while the string of the bag bit yet deeper into the hand of the other. 'No one could have done more. You were – heroic.' But she felt nothing, nothing at all. She was merely saying what she had to say, what the circumstances of this distraught woman standing among the stinking refuse bags and rubbish bins demanded of her. (In a remote past a bewildered Mrs Page was struggling over the first two syllables of 'disassociation'.)

'I just ... just ... I ... Now – how am I to manage without him now? How? How?'

'But you're free!' Lorna wanted to shout at her. 'You're free at last!' But that would have been no consolation. What Mrs Page was mourning was not so much the passing of the grub as the passing of her servitude to it. Lorna hugged the haggard, garishly overpainted woman closer to her, though never for a moment letting go of the bag with its terrible burden. 'You're still young,' she said. 'There's still – still ...' But she could not produce the silly, consoling clichés that she had so often produced on similar occasions in the past.

Mrs Page made an attempt to master her grief and at last got it under some semblance of control. 'Nanette's in there,' she sniffed, the back of a hand, the nails painted crimson, going to first one cheek and then the other in a wiping gesture. 'With him.'

'Oh, I'm glad you're not alone. That's good.'

'Would you like to come in and take a look at him?'

'Not now, I'm afraid. I'm – I'm on my way to a patient.'

'You've not got your car then?' Mrs Page scrutinized her, eyes narrowed, in what was probably disbelief.

Why hadn't she got the car? Why? She did not know. She had hurried out with the bag and had never thought of it. 'One of the tyres is flat,' she said. Mrs Page looked at her now with what seemed to be a growing hostility. 'And it's no distance at all.'

'The funeral's the day after tomorrow. Perhaps you could come to that. It's the Putney Crematorium. At three-thirty. The day after tomorrow.'

'I'll try to come, Mrs Page. I can't promise. It all depends on how many calls I have to make.' Mrs Page knew that she would not come. That was obvious, as she turned away now with a clicking sound at the back of her throat.

'Well, if you can manage it,' Mrs Page said. She began to mount the steps, many of which, Lorna could see now, were fissured and

165

chipped. She wobbled on her high heels at the top of them, the light through the crack of the front door picking out the boniness of one of her cheeks under the heavily mascaraed eye. 'I'd have liked you to see him,' she said in a hard, accusing voice. 'It's as if that illness of his had never been. He looks just as he used to look. Even Nanette noticed it. "But, Mum," she said, "it's Dad as once he was."' She shrugged: 'Well, if you're busy – if there's a patient waiting . . .'

'I'm sorry. Awfully sorry. But I will try –'

Before she could finish, Mrs Page had vanished into the house and closed the door behind her.

Lorna hurried on. I can feel nothing, nothing at all. Each time I used to visit him here or she came to see me or I saw her wheeling him around in that ghastly pram affair, it used to kill me. And now I feel nothing. *Nothing.* What's happened to me? What's the matter with me? I was a friend to that woman but tonight I might have been a stranger. Even a stranger might have felt more. *Disassociation . . .*

The wind became sharper as the bridge loomed up ahead of her. She began to walk out across it while, turbulent and polluted, the river flowed beneath. A car swished past, hurling her shadow out ahead of her; then another and another. She lifted the bag on to the parapet, resting it there as she looked first to her right and then to her left.

There was no one in sight. Far off, the lights of a car picked out the tops of the stunted trees that lined either side of the road down which she had walked. But that was still far away.

She gave the bag a push. She seemed to be pushing away a whole weight of years, almost a lifetime from her. The bag resisted, seemed a living thing as she struggled with it. Then it fell, plummeting down and down and down like a corpse into the black, rushing water.

35

Lorna stood at the kitchen window, a cup of coffee in one hand, and watched for the arrival of Mrs Emerson. She had thought of leaving a note either for her or for Matty and had then decided to wait. Unlike Matty, Mrs Emerson was always punctual; the wait could not possibly be for more than ten minutes at most.

The battered Jaguar car in which Mr Emerson often brought her to work on the mornings when he was not on an early shift, screeched to a halt. 'Ta-ta, love! Have a good day!' Mrs Emerson's skirt was high, revealing an expanse of plump thigh, as she struggled to get out of the front seat; her face was flushed.

Lorna went out to her as she began to clatter down the area steps.

Mrs Emerson looked up. 'You're bright and early!'

'I've got to go out to an urgent call. Could you please tell Dr Spencer – and try to keep them happy in the waiting-room?'

'You seem to have one urgent call after another. It's this weather. As soon as we have a bit of warmth and sun, things ought to improve. Who is it this time?'

'A new patient,' Lorna said, unable to think of anyone. 'Someone I've never seen before. A friend of a friend, so I didn't feel I could possibly say no.'

'He was driving even worse than usual this morning. Went through one red light after another. I can't think why I entrust my life to him.'

Lorna went back into the house, put on her coat and then, in case Mrs Emerson should see her from the basement, also picked up her medical bag. He had said not to come in the car; he would not be coming in his.

As she hurried along to the Green, her head lowered, someone greeted her: 'Good morning, Dr Martin. I was just popping over to see you.'

It was an elderly retired postmistress, a spinster, who spent much of her time 'popping over' with the most trivial of ailments or sometimes even with no ailments at all.

'I'll be back in a moment.'

This patient would never mind, however long she had to wait. She had often given up her place in the queue – 'You go ahead, dear. I've got the whole day before me.' Her only real illness, from which she would no doubt eventually die, was a tedium that no one would ever cure for her, least of all Matty or Lorna.

He had said that he would be seated on one of the benches round the Green and that she must pretend that their encounter was accidental; and, yes, there he was, with that cap pulled down low over his forehead and that scarf all but covering his mouth. He was wearing an overcoat that she had not seen before, beige-coloured with a collar of reddish fur.

She began to walk towards him without once actually looking at him until, at long last, she was some ten feet away. 'Mr Van Fleet!' Since there was no one in hearing, there was something absurd about the whole charade.

He indicated the space on the bench beside him, murmuring, 'Hello Lorna.' Once again she felt resentment that this man should call her by her Christian name.

She sat, placing the bag across her knees.

'What's in that?'

'It's my medical bag. I'm supposed to be out on a call.'

Now for the first time she looked at him closely and she was appalled by what she saw. That ultra-violet tan had a coppery sheen to it; there were deep grey-green shadows under his eyes, like fading, week-old bruises. His cheeks had caved in on either side of the gash-like mouth.

'Oh. I see.' His voice was husky.

'Have you some news of him?'

He shook his head, plunging his hands deep into the pockets of the expensive overcoat and hunching his shoulders as though he were chilled to the marrow.

'Oh, I'd hoped . . .' Her disappointment was like a child's. 'Then why did you want to see me?'

'There have been – developments.'

'Developments? What do you mean?'

'I don't know how to begin on all this. It's bloody difficult.' He turned to her and one of his eyelids quivered as though some grit had lodged beneath it. 'You see . . . when you telephoned to me – and when you waited for me outside the office that evening – I wasn't entirely frank with you. I'm sorry but I wasn't entirely frank with you. Perhaps I should have been – perhaps in the long run it would have been better – but at the time . . . Oh, this is so bloody difficult!'

'I think I know what you're trying to tell me about yourself and Bob,' Lorna said in a quiet, steely voice.

'You do? But how can you? Surely he never told you . . .'

Again the eyelid flickered and this time he put the back of a hand to it and began to rub.

'Bob *told* me nothing. But, as I said the other day, we didn't have to tell each other things, we don't now. We – well, we just know.'

'So you *knew*?'

Lorna nodded. 'All along.' The lie emerged with total conviction; at that moment she almost believed it herself and he certainly did. 'I knew what you meant about the *unconventionality* – wasn't that the word you used? – of his tastes, I knew exactly. And I knew that you shared them and that from time to time he was of, well, assistance to you.'

He stared at her now with a mingling of admiration, distaste and fear.

'And didn't that knowledge upset you – worry you?'

'Of course. That's why I called you and why I waited that day to see you.' She was wholly calm and businesslike. 'Anyway – what do you want me for now?'

He swallowed and the Adam's apple bounced up and down in the scrawny neck. 'They've been to see me,' he said in what was almost a whisper.

'They? Do you mean the police?'

He nodded. 'I wish to hell I knew how much they know. I wish I knew if he'd told them anything. He might have gone to them. Or they might have – broken him down.'

She saw now that he was not afraid for Bob – that he did not care a damn about Bob – but was afraid only for himself; and at that a sudden loathing of him spurted through her.

'If he were in this country – if he were in trouble here – I'd have heard from him,' she said.

'Not necessarily.'

'Of course!' Her tone, as the words wreathed out on the icy air, was bitingly contemptuous. 'If he were in any difficulty, he'd get in touch with me at once.'

He shrugged. For all her contempt and hatred for him, she could not help also feeling a certain pity that, previously so arrogantly in control of his destiny, he should now be so defence-less. It was no longer she who was seeking reassurance from him; their roles had been reversed.

'What did they ask you?'

'Oh, questions, questions. About myself. About him. About some of the people he brought to my house and some of the people I met at yours.'

'At mine!'

'When you were away.' He swallowed and again the prominent Adam's apple bobbed up and down in the long, scrawny neck. 'Fortunately – because of Avril and the children – I've never left any evidence of any kind lying around the house. So they found nothing, nothing at all.' He turned to her, voice and expression urgent: 'Is there anything of that kind – anything at all – in your house?'

She shook her head, suddenly remembering with total irrele-vance that this was the day of the funeral of the grub.

'Are you sure? Absolutely sure? It's vital that there should be nothing, nothing at all.'

'There's nothing.'

Evidently the quiet strength of her statement must have con-vinced him. 'Good.' She felt the terrible tautness of his body begin to loosen. 'Then it may be – it may be that that's the end of the story. I denied – of course – that anything criminal had happened. If Bob makes the same denial . . .' He stared at a stray mongrel that had streaked across the road in front of the oncoming traffic, and was now cocking a leg at the tree beside them. 'But what worries me is what the hell has happened to him!'

'It's strange that the police haven't been to the house. My house, I mean.'

'Yes. Yes. It's . . . Oh Christ I wish to hell I'd never met him. I wish to hell I'd never got mixed up in the whole bloody business.'

'Perhaps he wishes the same.'

There was a long silence, as the dog pattered away from them, weaving nose to ground, across the Green. Then he said:

'When he comes back – *if* he comes back – tell him to get in touch with me at once. *At once.* Or, no, *you* had better be the one to ring to arrange a meeting. And tell him to say nothing, give away nothing. Deny it all.'

Lorna got to her feet and stood over him, the medical-bag held in both her hands. 'How many were there?' she asked.

'How many?' He sounded astonished by the question. 'Christ, how the hell can I remember how many! Two or three were experienced little tarts. Not as young as they pretended to be. Two or three . . . Oh, what does it *matter*?'

'It may have mattered to them.'

He sank his chin yet deeper into his scarf and said nothing in reply.

'When I saw you here – in your car, several weeks ago – what were you doing?'

He did not answer, staring down at his shoes as though he had not heard her.

'Were you waiting for Bob?'

'No.'

'For someone else?'

'No.'

'Then . . .?'

'I was watching,' he said with sudden venom. '*Watching.* There's nothing illegal in that. Is there?'

'Watching? Watching what?' But as she spoke the question,

there came back to her a memory of those shrill cries and laughter as that group of girls had chased their ball through the gathering dusk. 'Oh, yes, of course!'

'Well, that isn't a crime, is it? Any more than it's a crime to take someone for a drive or to the cinema or to – to buy her sweets.'

'I swept up the papers.' She stooped lower over him, as though she were about to attack him, and visibly he shrank from her.

'Papers? What papers?'

'The sweet-papers. In the car. And your cigarette ends. Your Marlboro cigarette ends.'

'Do you mean to say . . .?'

'Bob was less careful than you. That's why I'm so frightened for him.' She straightened again and one hand released the bag, the other swinging it back and forth. 'Your wife,' she said. 'Does *she* know?'

'Thank God she's away at the moment. In the Bahamas. On a holiday.'

'I don't mean just about the police. Does she know about these – these rather special tastes of yours?'

His lips trembled but no sound emerged. Again the Adam's apple bobbed up and down in the scrawny neck. Then he said with a pathetic attempt at dignity: 'I don't see that that's any business of yours.'

'No. Perhaps not.' But Lorna knew now that that cold, almost silent woman had long been a party to his secret.

'I must get back to my patients,' she said.

'You won't forget what I said. If he comes back . . .'

'I know what to do,' she cut in brutally. 'I know exactly what to do.'

She began to hurry away from him with no word of goodbye, walking faster and faster as the traffic seemed to roar louder and louder in her ears and then through her whole body.

36

The Polish countess was in buoyant mood. 'I feel that soon, soon the spring will be here. During the winter months I think that maybe I will die. But now – now I can survive perhaps!'

'Of course you'll survive,' Lorna said wanly, not caring whether she survived or not. She raised the fine bone-china teacup to her lips – the countess herself was drinking out of one that was modern, cheap and thick – and sipped at the weak China tea that tasted like an infusion of hay.

'Do you remember that you say to me that I must not be afraid of going. I am not afraid! I tell you then – I am not afraid! But I am glad that I do not have to go – not yet.' She held out the plate that contained two Danish pastries sliced, as though each were a loaf of bread, into narrow slivers. 'Please.'

Lorna shook her head. 'Not another, thank you.' It was miraculous that this ancient, ailing woman, member of a once rich and powerful clan but now apparently without family and almost without friends and confined to this one-room basement flat, should none the less contrive to be so happy, even joyful.

'But you must eat! You do not look well. Excuse me if I say this – I should not say this to a doctor – but you do not look well. You are too thin. You must eat, you must eat!'

Lorna reached for her coat. 'I ought to be going. I have so many other calls.'

'No, no. First you must drink another cup of tea. And while you drink another cup of tea, I shall show you some photographs. Wait!' She had been used to commanding others; now she commanded Lorna, as she struggled up out of her chair and padded in her slippers to a desk. Her legs were monstrously swollen, her hands also swollen and purple.

She drew the photographs out of a brown-paper envelope,

dipping in one of those swollen, purple hands to extract what seemed to be an endless succession of yellowing snapshots, many frayed at the edges, of country houses and horses and dogs and people drinking or eating out on terraces or balconies while uniformed servants stood obsequiously behind them. 'This is my brother, Jan. He was killed in this last war. And this – this is my sister. She is also dead ... Ah, and here is Mamma, here is my darling mamma. She died when she was ninety-two, so perhaps I also can live to be ninety-two ...'

Lorna took one photograph after another and peered down, boredom and exasperation giving way, slowly, to a terrible sense of pathos. The country houses would now be museums; all these extravagantly dressed, overfed people, with their carriages and cars and guns and horses, were most, perhaps all, of them now dead; and the servants, once so eager to fulfil their most trivial whims, were now themselves the masters.

'And who is this?' The snapshot was of the head and shoulders of a young girl, with blond hair cascading down her back.

'But that is me, that is me! Ah, I was only thirteen then. Imagine! This friend of my father's took this photograph of me on my thirteenth birthday. How I remember that birthday! My father gave me this horse, and to me it was the most beautiful horse in the whole world. I do not think I have ever been so happy again. Yes, that was the happiest day of my life.'

But the girl had about her an air of wary vulnerability; perhaps she had not really been so happy as this old woman now remembered.

'You were very beautiful.'

'That is what they said. But you find it hard to believe now?' The countess laughed, throwing back her head to reveal her butter-yellow, ill-fitting false teeth. She had guessed precisely what Lorna had been thinking at that moment. 'They are all gone. And if I was beautiful then, then that has gone too. But I do not mind! Why should I mind? I have been happy, wonderfully happy. All my life I have been happy and even now I am happy.'

Lorna rose to her feet. 'Now I really must go. You have the prescription?'

'Yes, yes. Thank you. Tomorrow I will ask one of the two boys next door – they are very nice boys, very kind to me – to take it to the chemist's for me. I often talk to them about the past in Poland. They are always interested. Always. They call me "Auntie", you know.' There seemed to be an oblique reproach in this emphasis on her neighbours' interest, in contrast with Lorna's lack of it. 'I call them "boys", but one is fifty-one and the other is forty-seven!' Again she threw back her head and again the false teeth were revealed as she burst into joyous laughter.

'I'll come next week – the same time. Unless you need me before then.'

'No, no! Now the winter is ending. It is not necessary. I am not afraid of going, as you think – not at all. But not yet, not yet! I have some time yet!'

Forlorn and hungry, Lorna put her key into the front door of the house on her return from the Polish countess – she had lied and there had in fact been no other patients to visit, the countess was the last – and at once knew, feeling the certainty vibrating along her nerves, that when she opened the door there would be someone inside.

Fearfully, she slid in, switched on the light and then called 'Bob! Is that you? Are you back?' while the cat wreathed herself, purring, around her ankles. 'Bob!'

Then in the darkness above her his door opened and he said in a sleepy, cross voice: 'Yes. I'm back.'

She dropped her bag and began to hurry up the stairs. 'But what happened to you? Why did you never write? Why did you never telephone?'

He stood on the landing in nothing but vest and pants, his hands clasped before him; but it was not he but some fading, yellowing snapshot, like those of the Polish aristocrats long since dead or dying in exile. He might have been suffering from some terrible wasting illness, the once beautiful body now all jutting bones and the once beautiful face shrivelled, sunken, criss-crossed with a cobwebby hatching of wrinkles. He said nothing.

'Have you been ill?'

Mutely he shook his head.

'Oh, Bob, Bob!' She ran to him then and put her arms around him, smelling a sour-sweet odour that she knew well from the bedrooms of the mortally ill and feeling those bones hard against her. All at once he was sobbing, with a dry, retching sound, clutching her to him. Then, no less convulsively, he was pushing her away, retreating from her into his darkened room, an animal into its lair.

She followed him, putting a hand to the light. But he cried out 'No, no! Don't put that on!' and so she left it. A faint glimmer came through the window – he had not drawn the curtains – and slowly she made out in it the things that he had dropped about the room: clothes, his rucksack, a pair of shoes. That sour-sweet smell was now overpowering, nauseating.

He stood by the window, his face away from her so that all she could see of it was the light from outside glistening on a cheekbone.

'What *happened* to you?' Still he did not answer, standing totally motionless in his vest and pants. 'At least put on the fire.' She herself had begun to shiver uncontrollably.

At that he at last stirred himself, took a match-box in shaky fingers and lit the gas. Lorna moved towards the warmth as he retreated.

'What happened to you?' she repeated. 'Bob! Tell me!'

He shook his head.

'Did you go to Spain?' Silence. 'Did you?'

'No.' A dull monosyllable.

'Then what on earth . . .?'

'I – I travelled around. Just travelled around.'

'But where? *Where*?'

'Scotland mostly. Yorkshire. Northumberland.'

'Then why on earth didn't you get in touch with me? I've been ill with worry. I can't understand you.'

'No. I know.'

He had been gazing out of the window into the desolate garden; now he turned back and added fiercely: 'And don't try!' It was as if he had hit her in the face.

'Bob.' She advanced cautiously towards him, this wild animal that might at any moment spring on her. 'We've got to get things straight.'

'Oh, leave me! Leave me!' He raised both hands in a gesture of fending off.

'I've seen Harry Van Fleet.'

'Harry!'

'Twice. The first time it was I who insisted on seeing him – because I was so desperate for news. Then it was he who insisted on seeing me. He's been visited by the police.'

'Oh Christ!' He put both hands to his mouth, leaning forward, as though he were about to vomit.

'They've not been here. Yet. Perhaps they won't come. But he gave me a message for you. Two messages ... Bob, are you listening to me?' Motionless now, he was staring once again down into the garden. 'Bob!'

Mutely he nodded.

'First – he says on no account admit anything, anything at all. Deny, deny. Do you understand? And second – he wants to see you. But it's I who has to make the contact. I. Not you.'

He had taken the curtain beside him in both hands and was wringing it as though it were a piece of washing. 'What has he told you?' His voice was icy with despair.

'Nothing I didn't know already. Nothing I hadn't guessed. Or seen for myself. Or been told by Edie.'

'Edie!'

Suddenly he threw himself on the bed; then scrabbled at the bedclothes and got between them. 'Oh Christ! No! No!'

She went and sat on the edge of the bed and put the back of one hand against the cheek that was nearest to her. 'It doesn't matter. Don't you see? It doesn't matter. It doesn't matter, darling!'

But he had begun to burrow deeper and deeper into the bed, his head now under the bedclothes and his hands gripping at them so that, try though she might, tugging and jerking, she could not get them down.

Hopelessly she sat there while he now lay totally still under the covers, the animal shamming dead. Then in the same coaxing, wheedling voice that she had used to him as a child when, terrified or mortified by something that Dada had said to him or done to him, he had retreated from them all in precisely the same way, she told him: 'I'm going out for a moment. I'm going to go to the delicatessen and then to the wine-shop. We must celebrate your home-coming. You'd like some smoked salmon, wouldn't you? And I'll get some of that game pie you always like. And a nice claret. I haven't bothered to stock up since you went away. I've only got some plonk. I'll be back soon.' She touched his shoulder through the bedclothes and heard a muffled groan. 'Soon. Now pull yourself together and get yourself shaved and washed. Nothing's ever as bad as one thinks it is.' The trite words of comfort came back forlornly across the years. The thirteen-year-old girl was once again comforting her brother of six.

'Oh, Lorna! Lorna!' A hand emerged from under the bedclothes and sought her out. She felt it along her cheek, at her temple, then in her hair. 'What have I done? What have I done?'

She got off the bed. 'I'll only be away a little. Only a little.'

Returning with the smoked salmon, the wedge of game pie and the bottle of claret – she knew little about wine but the man in the shop had told her that it was their best – she suddenly felt an extraordinary elation. She had seen patients in the same state, even before premedication, as they awaited the surgeon's knife. She hummed to herself, one bag clutched to her while the other, containing the bottle, dangled from her hand. Later she would have to make contact with Harry Van Fleet and probe and coax until Bob had told her all his story. But both those things could be left for the morrow.

Opening the door, she called up the stairs in a voice that had become suddenly young and joyful: 'I'm back! I don't know whether you'll approve of this claret but Mr Golding said it was the ...' The silence closed around her, sealing her within it: the silence and her aloneness. Even the cat was no longer there.

'Bob!' she cried, racing up the stairs. 'Where are you? Bob!'

She looked from room to room. Crazily, she even opened both doors of the huge compactum out on the landing and peered beneath the high brass bedstead, where the tuck-box still rested, gathering dust to obliterate the prints of her fingers.

He had left nothing, no note, no sign. Only that terrible sweet-sour odour of mortality was heavy on the air; only the rumpled bedclothes showed where he had suffered his ignominious crucifixion.

Last she raced down the stairs, dragged open the door and looked out into the street. The cat scuttled in. The only other movement was that of a piece of paper caught against the gate. She went to it, stooped and retrieved it, surmising, wildly, that perhaps it held some message. But it was only a fragment of week-old newspaper, reeking of fish-and-chips.

37

'These are very serious offences. Of a particularly savage kind. That none of the victims has died is, well, frankly a miracle.'

The middle-aged, soft-voiced man, his short-cut grey hair divided with what looked like an incision diagonally across his head, reminded Lorna of a professor of anatomy whose lectures she had once attended. Beside him and a little behind him the young man with the sullen, scowling expression gnawed at a fingernail.

Lorna nodded. 'Yes. I realize that.'

'Any man who could do such a thing is, to my mind, sick as any of your patients.'

Again Lorna nodded, calm under the intensity of this quiet but devastating onslaught.

'You'd want to help such a man, wouldn't you? You'd want to get him treatment just as soon as possible?'

'But I've told you – I know nothing. Nothing.'

'Nothing.' He drew a handkerchief out of his pocket, blew first one nostril and then the other and carefully inspected the results before putting it away again. 'And your brother has been away for – what? – almost four weeks.'

'That's right.'

'And you've had absolutely no news of him? No letter? No telephone call?'

'Nothing. But there's nothing odd in that. Honestly there isn't. He often goes away like that, I've told you. That's the kind of life he leads.'

'The kind of life he leads.' He pondered a moment, waggling one of his outstretched legs from side to side. 'And you say that you've never had the least suspicion – indication . . .?'

'None whatever. If he were doing anything of that kind, I'd –

I'd be *bound* to know. He's lived with me off and on for years and years. And I've never, never once ... You can't be so close to a person and not know a thing like that.'

'You'd be surprised. It's often the closest who know the least.' He again unwrapped the brown-paper parcel on his lap. 'This anorak. You've never seen him wear it?'

Lorna gazed unflinchingly at the brown stains caked on the anorak, similar to those on the shirt, similar to those on that pathetic pair of knickers. 'This is the first time I've ever set eyes on it. It's the last thing he would wear. He's – well – very conservative in his clothes. He'd never wear a – a scarlet anorak with stripes like that. He *has* an anorak – I showed it to you upstairs. He's had it for years. Black. You saw for yourself.'

'Black. Yes.' He sighed.

'You've searched the whole house. You've seen for yourself. There's nothing, absolutely nothing. I just don't understand how you can possibly connect him with anything that ...' The young man with the frizzy orange hair continued to gnaw in silent absorption at that same fingernail, like a dog with a bone.

'Perhaps all this time he's had a room somewhere,' the older man ruminated.

'But I'd have known about that! And where would he have got the money from? Rooms aren't cheap in London. D'you know what he earned each week from that film-work of his?'

'He might have had other sources.' During the whole course of this long interview, he had never mentioned Harry Van Fleet but Lorna knew that it was of him that he was thinking.

'What other sources? What possible other sources?'

At last the older man rose and, still gnawing at that fingernail, the young man rose too.

'Thank you, Dr Martin. I'm sorry to have had to put you through this – this ordeal. But you do understand ... Apart from what has happened, there's always the possibility of other things happening in the future. We mustn't forget that. Oh, thank you.' She was handing him his umbrella. 'We can't leave a single stone unturned.'

'Well, of course not. But frankly ... I mean, the whole idea of my brother being involved in any way – it's so utterly absurd.'

He held the umbrella horizontally between both of his surprisingly muscular hands. 'If he should turn up – you will let us know at once, won't you?'

'Of course. I've – we've – nothing to hide. I'm sure he'll be only too willing to give you any help he can. But whether his help will be much use to you ...'

'You've been very patient.'

'Not at all. I'm afraid it's my patients who've been patient!'

His lips twitched briefly at her feeble joke. 'You won't forget. If you should hear from him – if he should come back here. You have my card?'

Lorna pointed to the hall-table.

'Good. Because, you see, one wouldn't want anything of that kind to be repeated. So one has to be extremely careful. And thorough.'

'Of course.'

Somehow, after that visit from the two detectives, Lorna managed to get through evening surgery. It was odd, almost miraculous, how one small part of one's mind could go on with its business of assessing symptoms, ticking up one against another and then coming up with its answers – a drug, a placebo, a decision to refer the case to a specialist, a few words of reassurance and sympathy – while all the time the major part of it was distracted by something wholly different. She was sure that, on balance, she had done her job as well that afternoon as on innumerable other ones and that her patients had been as satisfied as they would ever be; but if she had been asked whom she had seen or what action she had taken, she would have been unable to answer.

'Finished?'

She had hoped to work through her patients before Matty had worked through hers and so to avoid a confrontation.

'Yes. Finished. I feel whacked.'

'Poor darling. What a time you've been through.' Matty was struggling to her feet to come to Lorna where she had halted in the doorway. It was no longer possible to make an immediate escape. 'But I'm glad you've heard from Bob. That's one relief, isn't it?'

Lorna froze. She had forgotten that, before the visit of that afternoon, she had lied to Matty in order to stem the flood of her unending probing and sympathizing. 'Yes,' she agreed. 'Yes, it is.'

'Was it a letter or a telephone call?'

'A letter.'

'From Spain?'

'Yes.' She had answered both these questions already. Like that grey, quiet-voiced detective, Matty seemed determined to ask everything twice.

'Granada?'

Lorna nodded. 'But he said he was moving on.'

'No destination given?'

'None. He doesn't even know where he'll stop next.'

'It's so *odd*, pet.'

'Odd?'

'That long, long silence. Didn't he explain it?'

'Well, he'd been travelling in these remote places. And he did apparently send me two postcards but neither of them reached me, of course. I imagine that the posts in Spain are even worse than here.'

'You'd have thought he'd have put through a telephone call when he was in one of the big cities.'

'He's probably running through his money and wants to save what he's got. Well, you know what he's like, Matty.'

'It's because I *do* know what he's like that I find it all so – so baffling. I mean, he's so *close* to you. He's always been so close. He wouldn't go out on evenings when you were to be at home. And now to treat you like this . . . You didn't have a row, did you, pet?'

'No, Matty, we didn't have a row.'

'You're still worried. I can see that you're still worried. He's still on your mind. Why not take some valium?'

'You know that I only prescribe tranquillizers, I never take

183

them.' She had just, in fact, prescribed some more 'happiness pills' for a famished-looking, weepy Mrs Page.

'Why not come back and have a bite with Mother and me? We've a joint this evening. If the old girl's remembered to light the oven. It'll take your mind off things.'

'Sweet of you, Matty, But I – I feel done in. What I really need is a good night's sleep. I'm going to go straight to bed now, in fact. I just hope I don't get a call, that's all.'

'Well, have them referred to me. I'll do them for you.'

'Oh, no! I wouldn't dream of it. Things aren't as bad as all that.'

'Let me come upstairs then and get you your supper. You have a bath – there's nothing like a really hot bath to get one relaxed – and meanwhile I'll scramble you some eggs.'

'No, Matty. I'm all right. I'm *all right*!' The vexation she had been keeping under careful control broke through at last and her voice became all at once high and shrill. '*Please!*'

'As you wish, pet. I only wanted to be helpful.'

Lorna forced herself to put an arm round the other woman and give her a brief, placatory hug. 'You're very kind.'

'Oh, nonsense!'

Now it was Matty who was fretful. She turned and began to heave herself back towards her desk, only to swing round again with an agility amazing for someone so crippled. It was as though she were playing Anna's game of moving away in apparent indifference from some wounded mouse or bird and then all at once whipping round to pounce. 'Tell me, pet. Who were those two men?'

'Two men?'

'The ones that you were letting in as I was getting out of the car.'

'Oh, you've seen them before, I think. Or at least one of them – the older one. They run this local residents' association.' Only the previous evening a bearded young man from the association had called to extract a contribution. It was the first lie of which she could think.

'I didn't know there *was* an association.'

'Oh, yes. They're springing up everywhere now, aren't they?

They're particularly worried about what's happening round the Green.'

'I can't *remember* seeing either of them.'

'Well, I'm sure you have.'

'My memory's not as good as it was. I thought that perhaps they might be . . . friends of Bob's.'

'Why on earth should you have thought that?'

Matty shrugged, as she turned away again to lumber on towards her desk. 'Just a hunch,' she said. 'Just one of silly old Matty's hunches.'

38

Except on the rare occasions when he had a Saturday call, Bob usually accompanied Lorna on her weekend shopping trips. Her natural impulse was to go to the supermarket, since it was both nearest and cheapest, but Bob would always try to deflect her, saying that it was not merely crowded but crowded with such ghastly people, so dreary, so *predictable*. In the delicatessen, run by a diminutive Austrian Jew with a bushy grey moustache and side-whiskers that almost entirely obscured his face, Bob would press a Camembert gently with a thumb and then hold it to his nose to sniff at it. At the butcher's he would peer at the grain of the sirloin of beef on the counter before allowing Lorna to buy it for the Sunday joint. At the fishmonger's he would protest, 'Oh, no, not that cod again!' and point out to her the huge Scotch salmon on its catafalque of ice. It was, of course, invariably Lorna who paid for all these purchases, except on those rare occasions when he had, as he put it, 'had a good week' and insisted on buying some even more expensive luxury – a pot of caviare, a box of marrons glacés, a bottle of champagne or of vintage claret. As they walked home across the Green, Lorna would protest that they had spent far too much; at which Bob would link one arm in hers, the other swinging the overloaded shopping bag, and tell her that life was just not worth living unless one lived it recklessly.

That dictum, a favourite of his, now came back to her as, buffeted by the crowds in the supermarket, she struggled to remember what it was that she needed. At some time there had been a shopping list; but either she had left it back at home or else she had dropped it. Almost at random, she began to snatch at tins – baked beans, macaroni cheese, mushroom and tomato soup, sardines and luncheon meat: all the things that it was virtually impossible to persuade Bob to eat. Then, as she peered down into the wire basket, she was suddenly overcome with nausea at the prospect of all the lonely meals that stretched ahead of her, tin after tin opened and its contents tipped out into saucepan or plate, eventually to be forced somehow down her gullet. At that, she had a sudden, crazy impulse to upturn the basket and tumble everything in it on to the scuffed linoleum, the tins rolling about among the feet of the other astonished shoppers. But she checked herself, with the reminder 'Anna, I must remember Anna.' Last night there had been nothing for the Siamese to eat except a sausage from her own plate and Anna had rightly refused that after a few moments of sniffing at it in fastidious indignation.

'On your own today?' the woman at the cash-desk commented, as she rang up the purchases. She and Bob often bantered each other on the occasions when Lorna had succeeded in persuading him to enter the supermarket. Middle-aged and plump, with corrugated lips on which the lipstick formed a thick impasto, she had a way of leaning forward provocatively to take the purchases from the basket, her invariably low-cut dress falling away to reveal the swelling mounds of her ample breasts. But today she did not lean forward; she sounded faintly hostile, as she always did when Bob was not there.

'Yes, on my own.' Lorna attempted a smile, but it was more like a brief grimace.

As she crossed the Green, the strings of the two shopping bags cutting deep into her palms, she suddenly saw ahead of her a whole dreary succession of similar Saturday mornings, with the same panic buying, the same vaguely hostile and contemptuous 'On your own today?' and the same trudge, so easy in Bob's company and so effortful on her own, across the rectangle of threadbare grass and stunted trees, with a load of tins that would be pushed into a cupboard and probably never opened. Where was he? She felt, at that moment of acute despair and desolation, that she would never know, either now or in the future. Would he ever come back? *No.* That '*No*' was like a heavy stone that she carried round with her wherever she went and whatever she was doing. She could not push it away from her, as she had pushed that bag, weighted with a stone, into the turbulent river.

The cat whisked down the road towards her, from time to time scampering into a garden and then emerging out on to the pavement once again, her tail erect and her mouth opening and shutting as she emitted indignant squawk on squawk. It was as though she had already divined that there were four tins of cat food and some frozen liver in one of the shopping bags. 'All right, all right,' Lorna told her crossly. But the cat continued to squawk, wreathing herself between Lorna's legs and even trying to jump up at her.

There was a chipper little sports car, its hood back despite the cold of that day of early spring, parked in front of Lorna's own dust-streaked Hillman. Two people, a white girl and a black man with an Afro hair-style, were huddled against each other in it. Suddenly, with a shock, Lorna realized that the girl was Edie.

'Mother!'

'Edie!'

The cries were simultaneous; then Edie had tumbled out of the gleaming car and was hurrying towards the gate. She held it open, unsmiling.

'Darling! What a lovely surprise!' Lorna felt suddenly breathless. She might have run across the Green, instead of having plodded across it, her feet dragging and her head lowered. 'I'd no idea ... I thought you said ... Weren't you going away for the weekend?'

'Yes. I am going away. But I wanted to see you first.'

Lorna passed through the gate and Edie followed her, stooping and unhitching the strings of one of the two shopping bags from her mother's numb fingers. After a second of hesitation the cat brought up the rear.

'What about your friend?' Lorna half turned; and as she did so, music erupted from the tiny car, so loud that the step on which she was poised seemed to judder with it. The Negro's head was tilted back, as though no longer able to support the weight of all that hair; his eyes were shut.

'He's all right. Leave him. Has a hangover.'

'I'd have thought that din would make it worse.'

'Oh, don't say anything about the neighbours, Mother. Please!'

'I wasn't going to, dear.'

'It always used to be the neighbours – or the patients – when I put on a record. Remember?' Edie propped the shopping bag against the umbrella stand in the hall. 'It'll be all right there for the moment.'

'Oh, Anna might get at the liver. You know what a thief she is. Frozen. It might not be good for her. It won't take a moment to unpack the things.'

Edie sighed. 'Oh, very well. I don't know why you keep that cat. Seems to be nothing but trouble.'

'For company. One gets lonely from time to time.'

'How can one get lonely when one sees dozens of people every day?'

'Most of them are not people. They're just symptoms, that's all.'

'If you feel like that about them, shouldn't you pack it in?'

'Oh, I usually cure the symptoms. More often than Matty cures the people at any rate.'

They were now in the kitchen. Wearily Lorna began to remove the things from the bags and stow them away in the cupboards or refrigerator, while Edie watched intently, her hands deep in the pockets of her flared, scarlet trousers.

'Is he new?'

'Who?'

'That friend. The man with the sports car.'

'Oh, I've known him a week or two. He works at the Ghanaian Consulate. Very simple but fun.' Edie pulled out a chair and sat down in it heavily, as though all at once she felt tired.

Lorna shut the refrigerator door. 'I hope he drives carefully. He looks like the sort of person who mightn't.'

'Oh, he's careful enough. Too careful . . . Sit down, Mother.'

'I was going to get you a cup of coffee.'

'But I don't want a cup of coffee.'

'Well, I want a cup.'

'Later.' There was a compelling authority in the single word; Lorna's hand, outstretched to fetch down a cup, fell to her side. 'Sit, Mother.'

Lorna sat. She looked across at Edie, noticing or perhaps only imagining a new thickening and coarsening of the features, the lips seeming much fuller and more voluptuous, the jut of the chin more aggressive, the eyes brighter and more prominent, with a strained look to them as though from staring too long into a sunlit distance. She felt a chill of premonition.

'The police have been to see me.'

'The police?' For a brief moment Lorna managed to persuade herself that the police must have called about the pot that she knew that Edie and her friends smoked from time to time. But it was not that; even before Edie answered, she knew that it was not that.

'About Bob.'

'About Bob? Oh, but that's nothing to worry about!' Lorna was amazed by the quickness of her own defensive reaction. 'When I didn't hear from him for so long – when he seemed, well, just to vanish – I though that perhaps I'd better report it to them. So that they could make inquiries – at the hospitals and consulates abroad and so on. I'd become so anxious about him.'

'As well you might be.' Edie stared at her mother now, across the rough grain of the scrubbed kitchen table, with what seemed an intensity of hatred, though Lorna told herself, shocked and appalled, that no, no, it could not be that, it must only be apprehension and bewilderment. 'They made *me* anxious.'

'What did they say?'

'It's not what *they* said that's important, it's what *I* said. I thought I ought to tell you, Mother. Warn you. It seemed only fair.' A forefinger, the long nail looking to Lorna as though it had been dipped in blood, traced one of the deep, greyish grooves across the surface of the table. 'I told the truth.'

'The truth? What truth?'

'They wanted to know everything I knew about Bob.' The forefinger was now tracing another deep, greyish groove; it stopped and picked at it. 'Everything. And I told them.'

'Edie! What *do* you mean?' Suddenly and strangely Lorna again had a vision of an upturned shopping basket and tins rolling in all directions among the feet of anonymously hostile strangers.

'I *had* to tell them. I'm sorry, Mother, but there was no other way.' She looked up; and having spoken so softly until now, she demanded loudly and harshly: 'Why the hell didn't you tell me? Warn me?'

'Tell you? Warn you? What do you mean?' Lorna was attempting to pick her way among and over those cascading and rolling tins. She was stumbling, tripping, falling.

'You knew. They'd been to see you. And you never told me. You never picked up the telephone and told me. You never told me when I rang. You never asked me to come round. You never asked for my help.' That last was the deepest grievance of all, Lorna knew.

'I . . . I couldn't, dear. I . . . didn't want to involve . . .'

'But I *am* involved. Already. I've always been involved. In a sense, I'm more involved than you have ever been or ever will be.'

Lorna got up, her body feeling bruised and stiff as though from that imagined fall among the cascadng tins, took down a tin of cat food and began to open it. The air was suddenly permeated by the nauseating smell of fish. Anna let out what was almost a human squeak of pleasure and put out a paw to tug at Lorna's skirt, a claw entangled in its threads.

'One has a loyalty,' she said stonily. 'He's my brother, Edie.'

'Oh, more than that. Much more than that.' Edie tossed back her thick, shiny hair, her face suddenly predatory and cruel as it caught the shaft of winter sunlight that lanced through the window.

'What do you mean by that?'

Edie shrugged. Then: 'You know where he is.' It was a statement, not a question.

Lorna emptied the tin into a saucer, shaking it so violently that some fragments from it spattered the sleeve of her jacket. But she did not notice. She stooped to put the saucer down before the loudly purring cat. Then, her body still stiff and aching as though from a fall, she straightened herself. 'No, I don't know where he is. I wish I did but I don't. I just don't. I have no idea, no idea at all.' There was something implacable, even murderous about both her tone and her gaze as, the empty tin in one hand and the tin-opener in the other, she walked over to her daughter and then leant over her. Edie cringed, twisted sideways, almost rose. 'But if I did have any idea, I'd never tell them. Or you. Or anyone.'

Edie pushed back her chair, its shriek as its legs slid across the tiles making the startled cat look up from the saucer with a round, unwinking gaze. 'I believe you,' she said. 'I really believe you.' Her tone was one of wonder; for the first time she had realized the full extent of her mother's love. 'Yes.' She began to retreat backwards towards the door; then she halted, immobile in the shadows at one end of the kitchen as Lorna now stood immobile in the shadows at the other, with that single shaft of wintry sunlight between them. 'But you're crazy, Mother. Quite crazy. What's the use? How does it help him? How *can* it help him?'

'One can't betray people. Not the people one loves.'

'But it's not *betraying* him! For God's sake, Mother! Like they said, like they told me – he's sick, he needs help, medical treatment, psychiatric treatment.'

Lorna shrank, her head sinking between her raised shoulders and her knees buckling. She remained upright only by an effort of the will. 'I don't know. I just don't know.'

Abruptly, so abruptly that Lorna gave a small, startled gasp, as though she thought that her daughter were about to assault her, Edie moved back to the table and stooped to retrieve her bag. 'Don't be so idiotic!' she cried out. A hand plunged downwards and came out brandishing a sheaf of newspaper cuttings. 'Look at these!'

Lorna jerked her head away, like one of her child-patients refusing a thermometer or a dose of medicine.

'Look!'

'I don't want to look. All that – all that may have nothing to do with him. Nothing at all. '

'But it *may* have. It very likely may have.' She thrust the wad of cuttings at her mother but still Lorna refused to take them from her, much less to look at them. 'It's his sort of thing. Exactly his sort of thing.'

Lorna began to cry, with loud, tearing sobs, her chin lowered on to her breast-bone and her hands over her ears as though in an attempt to shut out this inexorable voice above and beside her.

Merciless, Edie went on, her voice acquiring a strange ring of triumph at the total humiliation of her mother before her eyes: 'There was this woman on television. She was talking about it, talking about her daughter. She was a very ordinary sort of woman, not even a very nice sort of woman. One felt that, though part of her was horrified and grief-stricken, another part was really enjoying it all – the attention from the neighbours, the newspaper-men, television cameras. But I felt for her, I really felt for her. I mean, it was almost as though it were me in that ridiculous pair of ear-rings that she'd put on and that dreadful flowered apron that she'd forgotten to take off. And Harry – he was watching with me – Harry, that Ghanaian, said. "If I ever got my hands on a bastard that could do a thing like that, I'd throttle him there and then." That's what he said. Those were his exact words.'

Lorna went on sobbing, doubled up now, while at her feet, totally unconcerned, the cat fastidiously licked the rim of the saucer. All at once Edie crossed to her and attempted to put an arm round her shaking shoulders; but Lorna savagely pulled away. 'I'm sorry,' Edie said, now contrite and pitying. She shrugged, hands again deep in the pockets of the scarlet trousers. 'I'm sorry, Mother. I can't expect you to see it as I see it – as any normal person must see it. I just don't understand . . .' She broke off; she would never understand and she knew that she would never do so. 'Well, I suppose I'd better go.'

She went out of the kitchen and Lorna followed, to say behind her in the hall: 'How did they know?' Her voice, fearful and plaintive, sounded like a child's.

'How did they know what?'

'Where to find you.'

'Matty told them.'

'Matty!'

Edie nodded, her back to her mother as she first thrust the newspaper cuttings back into her bag and then adjusted the strap of the bag on her shoulder.

'Then they must have seen Matty too.'

'Yes.'

'She never told me. I'd no idea.'

Again Edie shrugged. Then she turned round and put out both her arms, in a reversal of roles that turned her into the comforting, all-powerful mother and Lorna into the distracted, suffering child. 'Oh, Mother! Mother! If only I could help you!'

Lorna did not run into the arms extended to her. Instead, she stiffened, took a pace backwards, frowned down at the hands that she was holding clasped before her. 'I don't need any help,' she said in a calm, steely voice.

'Well . . .' Edie turned and opened the front door. She stood on the steps for a moment, as though undecided whether to stay with her mother or to join the young man asleep, mouth open, in the car. The whole street was still juddering to the raucous music.

Lorna stepped forward behind Edie. In a momentary impulse, similar to that when she had stood on the pavement with one of her hands on the handle of the pram in which the grub had lain outstretched and had all but pushed it out into the speeding traffic, she now all but thrust a hand between her daughter's averted shoulder-blades and sent her headlong down the steps on to the gravel below. Then, appalled, she drew back. 'I'm sorry, Edie,' she said in what was almost a whisper; though whether she was apologizing for that sudden murderous impulse or for a devotion to her brother so much more profound than she could feel for this child of hers, she did not then know nor would she ever know.

'I'm sorry too, Mother.' Briefly, Edie turned; briefly she kissed her mother on a hot, tear-stained cheek.

Then she was running down the steps and out towards the sunlight, the blaring music, the chipper little car, her shiny, sleepy lover.

Lorna did not wait to see the departure of the car; but standing by the paraffin heater in the dim, untidy hall, she listened for the din of its engine and that raucous music to fade into silence. As soon as she had closed the door, she had been overcome by a terrible lassitude. She thought of the cup of coffee that she had promised herself but it seemed too much effort to go into the kitchen, to fill and put on the kettle, to fetch down cup and saucer, to measure out the powder. She wandered into the sitting-room and, shivering with the cold, stooped to light the gas fire. For a while she knelt before it, hands outstretched, until her palms began to tingle and her face to burn and dry. She wished now that she had responded to those outstretched arms and that cry of 'If only I could help you!' That was what had always been wrong with all her relationships, not merely with Edie but with others. It was she who must always be the one who offered assistance, encouragement or comfort; the doctor could never bear to be the patient, the mother to be the child.

She switched on the television set – the first time she had ever done so in the morning – and then went and tugged the curtains across, so that the long, narrow room, once two small ones now knocked into one, became soothingly shadowy. She thought of Bob pulling the bedclothes over his head and burrowing deeper and deeper; she was making the same kind of cocoon for herself. With a groan she stretched out on the sofa, her position ungainly, skirt rucked above her knees and one shoe half off while the other lay on the floor. She stared at the screen. Two puppets, a dog and a duck, moved their heads jerkily from side to side as they talked, the dog in a deliberate *basso profundo*, the duck with staccato quacks. She shut her eyes. The absurd dialogue was somehow as soothing as the drawn curtains and the warmth radiating from the fire in front of her.

She wished that Edie were back with her now; but the Edie to whom she craved to pour out her pleadings, explanations and apologies was not that same Edie who had run down the steps, her bell of glossy, blond hair swinging from side to side, to that car, improbably open in this chill of early spring, and her lover waiting in it; but rather the Edie who had been a schoolgirl, always docile, sometimes even cowed, with her worries about being too fat, her unpopularity with one of her form-mistresses and her tendency to begin to blush suddenly for no apparent reason. But that Edie was gone for ever – destroyed by time and experience and (yes, she had to face it) Bob.

As Lorna unwillingly acknowledged that to herself, tearing the admission of it out of some dark, aching recess at the centre of her being, she became disagreeably conscious of a faint sweet-sour odour, similar to that odour that had hung about Bob's dishevelled, unwashed presence on the last occasion that she had seen him. Where did it come from? She raised one hand to her nostrils and then the other. When she raised the second hand, she noticed the fragments of cat food on her sleeve. But this smell was different from that. It was like the ghost of a smell, come back to haunt her without the presence to which it belonged. She felt first troubled and then panic-stricken, sitting bolt upright on the sofa, looking about her and finally getting to her feet. She climbed the stairs to the bathroom, one hand on the rail as though to help drag herself out of some dark, viscous pit. She went to the wash-basin, dazzled by the sunlight after the gloom of the curtained sitting-room, and turned on the tap. She soaped her hands and then even the wrists and the forearms above them, peeling back the sleeves; and then she began to rinse, the water trickling to the elbows as she stooped, now right and now left, over the basin. There was a curious kind of absolution in this process, as though she were washing away all the mutual resentments between herself and Edie, their misunderstandings, quarrels, bitter exchanges of words. Then, for a brief, dizzying moment of total disorientation, it was not she, a tired, worried, middle-aged woman who was washing her hands at the basin, but Bob; and she, disquieted and puzzled, was looking on. 'Why do you do that?' 'Do what?' 'Keep washing your hands.' 'I like them to be clean.' 'But they are clean. Already.' 'Then I suppose that the psychiatrists would say that I was trying to wash away some guilt . . .'

She snatched a towel from its rail and hurried out of the bathroom, leaving both obsessive washer and obsessive watcher behind her. She dried her hands on the landing with quick, fretful gestures and then threw the damp towel over the banisters. It slipped to the floor and she did not attempt to pick it up. Suddenly she thought of Matty, who had been visited by the police, who had betrayed Edie's address to them but who had never said anything of all this to her. She remembered how, watching from the window while Matty struggled to release herself from the three-wheeler, her face red and shiny with sweat and one crutch sticking out of the door like the antenna of some giant insect, Bob had given a fastidious shudder and then said: 'It's as though one were watching a chrysalis hatching out. But what emerges is not a butterfly but something that one can hardly bear to look at.' Lorna had been shocked; and she had been even more shocked when, after she had remonstrated with him, he had then gone on: 'Sometimes I really hate her for being such a *mess*.' 'How can you possibly hate the poor dear for something that is no fault of hers?' Lorna had cried out. But now she, too, felt that same fastidious recoil; she, too, hated Matty.

She began to run down the stairs, snatched up her overcoat and bag from the chair where she had thrown them, and hurried from the house. The car coughed and spluttered, just as the elderly, retired postmistress, now at last triumphantly suffering from some ailment that was not imaginary, had coughed and spluttered her germs over the other waiting patients that morning. Then at last resentfully it came to life.

Matty opened the front door. 'Hello, pet! What a lovely surprise!'

The poodle waddled down the corridor and began to sniff at one of Lorna's ankles. Matty was in a butcher's apron, with a scarf wound around her head. The scarf had the effect of making her head look even more disproportionately large for the misshapen body.

'I wanted a word with you.'

The small eyes squinted at Lorna with incipient alarm. 'Well, of course, pet! Come in! You know you're always more than welcome. I've just been washing the old girl's hair – my weekly chore. And now I'm drying it for her. Come in! Come in!' The poodle, having given up its sniffing, was now scratching lethargically at one of its ears in the middle of the passage. 'Oh, Kiki, do get out of the way!' Matty gave the dog a gentle nudge with the toe of her slipper, at which it let out a squeal.

'What are you doing to Kiki?' Mrs Spencer demanded angrily from the sitting-room.

'Nothing, Mother, nothing at all.'

The old woman sat in her dressing-gown on a straight-backed

chair, sodden wisps of hair sticking to her neck, forehead and cheeks. A drier lay on the floor beside her.

'Hello, Lorna. Wish you didn't have to see me like this. I know I look a fright. No need to stare so hard, dear.'

Lorna gave herself a little shake. 'Was I staring? Sorry.' She sank on to the sofa.

'Take off your coat,' Matty said, picking up the hair-drier in one hand and the comb in the other. 'It's far too hot in here but that's how Mother likes it, as you know.'

Lorna struggled out of her coat, without getting off the sofa; then she watched as Matty tugged the comb with vicious jerks through the scant, tangled hair. From time to time the old woman let out a little gasp or a squeal that sounded exactly like Kiki's; once she even protested, 'Oh, don't be so rough! Do you want to scalp me?'

'She's like a child,' Matty looked up to say. 'Just like a child. Isn't she?' White strands of hair trailed from the comb; the drier hummed.

At last Matty had finished. The old woman got stiffly to her feet. 'You and Matty want a private talk,' she said. How had she known? Unless Matty had told her of the visit from the police. But, as the old woman was always complaining, Matty told her little or nothing. 'I'll go and peel the potatoes. It's something Matty hates doing – she will buy them in tins or as that horrid powder.'

Matty began to wind up the cord of the hair-drier, leaning against one of the battered armchairs, its seat stained and covered with dog-hair, with one crutch under an arm and the other propped against a corner behind her. She seemed to be wholly absorbed in this task, as though no longer aware of Lorna's presence.

Lorna leant forward on the sofa. 'Matty – why didn't you tell me?'

'Tell you? Tell you what, pet?' Now she was heaving herself over to a built-in cupboard and putting the hair-drier on to one of the shelves, her red, shiny face averted and her close-cut grey hair glistening with sweat at the nape of her neck.

'The police. Edie told me that you'd sent them to see her. You should have told me, Matty.'

'I didn't *send* them to see her. Let's be accurate. They wanted to know if you had any close relatives and so I felt I must ... If I hadn't given them her address, then Mrs E. would have done so, I'm sure.'

'Did they question Mrs E.?' Lorna was appalled.

'Yes, dear. They called that afternoon – after surgery – when you had that emergency from your Polish countess. Thursday, was it?'

'But why didn't you *tell* me? Why, Matty? Why? I just don't get it.'

Matty sank into the sofa beside Lorna, tightening the knot of the butcher's apron. 'There seemed no point in worrying you, when you were distracted enough with worry already, God knows. Was there? Mrs E. and I agreed on that. They didn't stay very long. And there was really nothing I could tell them.'

'What did they want to know?'

'Where he was. Whether we'd seen him around. That kind of thing. They weren't very communicative. Not at all. Just said they wanted to trace him. They *did* ask if I'd noticed the people he'd entertained while you were away but I told them that I was never at the surgery after seven and that I'd seen absolutely no one. Oh, and of course I said nothing about the letter either, pet.'

'The letter?'

'The one you had from him the other day. From Spain.'

Lorna almost cried out 'But that was a lie! There *was* no letter. I only invented one to stop your endless prying!' But she was still too distrustful of Matty, for all her protestations of loyalty and discretion, to make that confession. 'Oh, thank you, Matty. But you could have been completely frank with them. It wouldn't have mattered. Why should it?'

'What do they want him for?' Matty edged closer, her strong, spatulate fingers once again at the knot to the butcher's apron.

'I don't know, Matty. Honestly. They told me no more than they told you. Nothing important, they said – routine inquiries was the phrase, if I remember rightly. I suppose he's done something silly once again. The car perhaps – or that wretched motorbike of his. You know how secretive he is.'

'Yes, I know.' Matty stared at Lorna with an appraising, almost baleful scrutiny.

Lorna knew that she had not been believed. Avoiding Matty's gaze, she said: 'I wish he'd come back. Or write again.'

Matty sighed. 'He's never been anything but a worry to you.'

'Well, I suppose that your mother's never been anything but a worry to you, Matty. But you wouldn't want to be without her, would you?'

'Oh, I don't know,' Matty said indifferently. 'I really sometimes wonder.'

'I do wish you hadn't put them on to Edie. It upset her no end.'

'I've already told you, pet – if I hadn't given them the address, Mrs E. would have done so. Or they'd have found some other way to get it. If they'd asked you, you'd have had to give it, wouldn't you?'

Lorna drew a long sigh. 'I suppose so, Matty. Yes.'

'I hope he hasn't done anything . . .' Matty's voice trailed away. 'One hasn't an inkling of what goes on behind that charming façade of his.'

'I think I've a pretty good idea. We don't conceal things from each other – not important things.' She had already forgotten that only a little while before she had described Bob as secretive.

'Poor Lorna.'

Lorna gave a small, hysterical laugh. 'Why do you and Edie always have to call me "poor"?'

'I suppose because we both love you, pet. And because we both feel deeply sorry for you.'

'I don't want you to feel sorry for me – either of you. It's the last thing I want.'

There was a silence. Lorna, stiff and unyielding, stared straight ahead of her at the fan of yellowing paper that stood, slightly askew, in the empty hearth. Then, all at once, she felt Matty's hand at her temple, fingering her hair.

'You should take more care of your hair,' Matty said. 'Why don't you let me give you a shampoo and set, like Mother's? The water's beautifully hot, you know. And I have this special oil shampoo – just what you need for those split ends of yours. You and Mother have the same kind of hair. Dry.'

Lorna jumped to her feet. 'I haven't time, Matty. Not now. I've so much to do. And you'll be wanting your lunch. Another time.'

'Why not stay and have a bite with us?'

'It's awfully kind of you. But I've honestly got no appetite. I'll just have a biscuit and a cup of coffee back at home.'

'As you wish, pet.' Matty began to lumber up, with effortful jerks of her torso. Lorna stooped to help her, handing her first the crutch beside her and then the one in the corner. 'There's always another time.' As always, Matty was annoyed, rather than grateful, to be assisted. Breathing stertorously, she followed Lorna out into the hall. 'Now don't be peeved with your old friend Matty. She only didn't want to tell you about the police because she didn't want to make you more worried. She acted from the best intentions. You must really believe that, pet.'

'Yes, Matty. Thank you.'

One of the crutches struck Lorna's ankle as Matty edged nearer. 'You know you can always rely on me. Confide in me. I'd do anything – anything in the world – for you. At any time. Anywhere.' The last words came out punctuated by gasps as she now dragged herself behind Lorna to the front door and out on to the steps.

'Yes, I know, Matty. I know. And I'm very grateful.' But the truth was that she felt no gratitude at all, only a totally inexplicable and corrosive resentment.

'Shall I say goodbye to the old girl for you?'

'Oh, yes, please. I forgot.'

'And if you have any news of him, you'll let me know at once. Won't you, pet?'

'Yes, Matty. Of course. I'll let you know.'

'Now chin up, pet! Don't look so depressed!'

39

Three days later Lorna dreamed uneasily in the empty and silent house, the cat curled up in the crook of one arm while the other lay across her face as though in anticipation of a sudden blow. She and Bob, children once again, were cooking sausages on the fire that he had kindled beside his tent at the bottom of the garden. He picked one out of the frying-pan on the end of a fork and, happy and laughing, held it out to her; but as her nostrils filled with the horrible sweet-sour stench of it – no, it should not smell like that, no, no – she shrank away first in unease and then in growing horror. Now he was pushing the sausage at her, closer and closer, while the fire roared and crackled. Either she must take it from him or retreat into the fire . . .

She awoke, with a gasp and then a small whimper, to the sound of the telephone ringing beside the bed.

'Yes?' Her fingers were tingling as they held the receiver. She heard the peep-peep-peep of a call-box telephone and repeated 'Yes? Yes?'

'Lorna? Is that you? Lorna?' She could not believe it. It was the voice of that boy beside his tent, speaking to her, young and tentative, across the years.

'Bob!' It was a cry of anguish and longing.

'Listen carefully. Listen. I need you. You've got to help me.'

'But where are you? Where?'

'Listen. I'm on the Green. Yes. The Green. I daren't come to the house. Do you understand? I want you to come here. Now. At once.'

'Yes. Yes, of course. But, Bob . . .'

He had rung off.

She scrambled out of bed and began to pull on her clothes in a frenzy. She must take her medical bag, she must not forget that.

Otherwise the two watchers in the front of the house and the two behind it – she was sure that they were watchers, even though the cars changed and the people in them changed – might guess at her rendezvous. She must be careful, very, very careful. On no account must she lead them to him.

As she opened the front door on to the icy, wind-swept night, Anna whisked out ahead of her and streaked across the road, no doubt to some tryst of her own. Yes, there was that deep coral Fiat, an exotic bug on wheels, with the young man and woman seated in it as they had been once before. No doubt she – or Bob, if he were to turn up – was expected to dismiss them as a courting couple. But she knew better, oh, she knew better.

With extreme casualness, pausing to look into the bag under the lamp-post in a pretence of making sure that she had all she needed with her, she walked down the pavement and then crossed the road to her car. The engine died on her, not once but repeatedly; and then, realizing that in her panic she had flooded the carburettor, she had to wait for what seemed many minutes until it had drained. At long last she managed to get away; and, looking in the mirror, she felt an intense relief that the couple were not following. She had been out on a number of calls these last three nights, one of them to Mrs Page who had swallowed an ineffectual number of aspirins in a pretence of trying to kill herself. That was lucky. They had got used to her leaving the house in the middle of the night.

She looked at her watch: twenty past two. And with that knowledge there swept over her a sudden overwhelming desire to sleep, sleep, sleep, to go on sleeping into a future in which everything would once again be as it used to be, with her and Bob and Edie sharing the life of the house that had then seemed so much less narrow and so much less dark and so much less shabby.

He was seated on the same bench on which Harry Van Fleet had been seated; but at first, with that stubble on his face, his shoulders hunched like those of an old man and his eyes closed – surely he could not be asleep? – she hardly recognized him. The rucksack was on the ground beside him; she could see no sign of the motorbicycle just as there had been none when he had come back so briefly to the house. Perhaps he had sold it.

'Bob!'

The eyes opened with a crazed, startled expression as though he did not know who this was calling out to him. Then he got to his feet with the slowness of someone picking himself up after a jolting fall, swayed slightly before her as though to fall again and at last advanced. 'Good girl,' he said in a voice that was not the voice that she had known in recent years but a voice youthful and hesitant, the voice she had heard on the telephone, totally at variance with his old man's appearance.

'What have you been doing? Why did you run away like that? It was the worst thing you could have done. Of course that only makes them more suspicious.'

She scolded him, as once she used to do, and as in the past the colour mounted under the greyish stubble, he hung his head, said nothing.

'They realize you're sick,' she said. 'They know that. If you come back with me, we can get some help for you. It's – it's like an illness. You're not to blame for it. They know that.'

'Oh, for Christ's sake, Lorna!' Suddenly it was the other Bob, the Bob who was secretive with her and who had told her lies and evasions and who had known Harry Van Fleet and had been in that horrible complicity with him. 'Shut up! Don't talk such utter *balls*!'

She stared at him aghast.

'They'd lock me up,' he said. 'For years and years. Perhaps for ever. Do you realize that? Perhaps for ever. And I just couldn't take it. No.' He shook his head. '*No.*'

'Then what are you going to do?'

'You must help me. Please. Please, Lorna! I can't do it. Not to myself. I can do terrible things to other people but not to myself. You must help me. You've always helped me. Whatever Dada said, whatever anyone said, you've always helped me.' Suddenly his voice had taken on the pleading, wheedling tone that she had learned to know so well: coming up the stairs and walking past his door or in hotel rooms on their holidays together or once during a picnic when he felt himself slipping into a coma. 'Please! Please, Lorna!'

'I ... I don't ... can't ...' But she knew that she would do whatever he asked of her, as she had always done.

'Come!'

He put out a hand, grey and greasy with dirt, and took her hand brutally in his, the long nails digging like talons into the palm.

'But where? Where? What do you want?'

He shouldered the rucksack with one arm while the hand of the other still gripped her close. They began to cross the Green.

Now they were walking in total silence, a tramp holding the hand of a well-dressed, middle-aged woman, down that same road, a funnel for the icy wind off the river, that she had taken, past Mrs Page's house, to the bridge. They passed Mrs Page's house, dark under overhanging trees, and a number of similar huge, dilapidated houses, teeming now with students and immigrants, until at last they came to one house, its windows boarded up and its drive overgrown with weeds, with a notice-board to say that it was about to be demolished so that a block of flats could be erected in its place. He walked round the side of this near-ruin and Lorna all but tripped over a tussock of grass as, their hands still joined in that ferocious clasp, she had to follow him. Evidently he had been here before and knew his way.

A cobweb strayed over her face and in panic she clawed it away from her with her free hand, at the same moment that he pushed at a door that led round the side of the house into a wilderness of a garden.

'Where are we going? What are you doing?' Now at last she spoke.

There was a shed beside what had once been the back door to this Victorian mansion and without making any answer, Bob pushed at its door too, pushed and pushed again, until it yielded and creaked open. The moonlight shone on a lavatory bowl without a seat, with bags of cement stacked round it.

Silently he opened his rucksack and got out a syringe and four capsules of insulin. Silently he filled the syringe, throwing empty capsule after capsule into the wilderness beyond them. Then he beckoned her into the shed, which he had already entered himself.

One hand held the syringe while the other went to his trousers. The trousers fell about his ankles revealing legs such as she had seen in the terminal wards of hospitals. He sat down on the lavatory bowl, wrapped the end of the syringe with extreme care in one corner of his shirt and then whispered: 'Do it for me, Lorna. I can't do it for myself. Please! But don't get your fingerprints on it. On no account get your fingerprints on it.'

She bent over him. He put up one skeletal arm and then the other around her neck, and she was overcome by the sweet-sour stench as though by ether. She could hardly move; she was suffocating. But she forced herself on. She took the syringe, wrapped in the end of the shirt, and she did as he said, taking every care to see that her fingers never touched it. His lips came up to hers, like a baby's sucking at the breast.

'Oh, Bob! Bob!' One of her tears splashed on to his upturned face.

'Quick! Oh, quick!' Again the lips sought hers.

With one hand she felt for his shrunken thigh. Then with the other she plunged the needle home.

'Thank you,' he said on a sigh. Then: 'Now go, Lorna. Go!'

His trousers still around his ankles, still seated on the glimmering bowl, he took the syringe from her unwilling hand and flung it in a wide arc into the former garden. 'Go!' he shouted.

Lorna began to run.

40

In the curtained bedroom – outside the weak afternoon sunlight was warming the spikes of the early bulbs that Bob had planted there – Matty crooned over Lorna like a mother over an ailing child. 'Rest, sweetie. Rest! Let go! I can take care of everything until that boy gets back from his rugger tour. Matty may be an old crock but she can still put in a full day's work – and some overtime. *Rest!*'

Lorna stared up at the ceiling as she tore at the corner of a handkerchief with her teeth.

'Soon that valium will take effect. You'll see. Any moment now. I know you didn't want me to give you the injection but, after all, this is no ordinary situation. Anyone, anyone in the world, would need a tranquilliser when faced with a thing like this.'

The tears began to well out of Lorna's eyes and then trickle down her cheeks. But she made not a sound. Matty took her hand; but this grip was soft and gentle, not like that other grip when she and Bob hurried down that funnel for the icy wind.

'Perhaps it's for the best. I know that's a hard thing to say and perhaps I shouldn't be saying it to you now. But perhaps it is for the best.' Lorna gave a little whimper; if only she could somehow stop this crooning, coaxing voice, its words dripping over her like syrup! 'After all, what sort of life would it have been for him, shut away for years and years? Because it *would* have been years and years, it would have *had* to be years and years. He'd have loathed that. Among a lot of other people who'd also –'

'Matty! Please! *Please!*'

'Sorry, pet. Matty only wants to console you. To see you your old self again.' She gave the hand she held a sudden, small painful squeeze and then let go of it. 'Now you shut your eyes and I'm going to try to put this room of yours into some sort of order. It's not like you to let it get into this sort of mess. Shut your eyes, pet.'

Lorna shut them. But she could still hear Matty, as she blundered and heaved herself around the room, breathing effortfully. The door of the cupboard creaked open, to be followed by a drawer. Then there was a crisp folding of paper as *The Times* was collected off the carpet.

'Matty! It's not necessary! Please!'

Lorna now opened her eyes again. Matty was at her dressing-table, using her comb to drag the fine, greying hairs off her brush. Her mouth was clamped together as, leaning against the wall for support, she scraped and tugged. 'I'd better give this a wash for you,' she murmured. Then in the same tone of voice, almost inaudible and expressionless, as though she were talking not to Lorna but to herself, she went on: 'How you adored that brother of yours! I think you'd have done anything he asked of you. Anything at all. He'd only to say the word.'

Lorna stared up at the ceiling, her body rigid and her hands clenched along her sides. She was certain now that Matty knew, knew it all; and she was equally certain that no one else would ever know.

'Now go to sleep, pet! Sleep!' the voice began crooning once again. 'Shut it all out of your mind! . . . And when you wake, then perhaps Matty'll give you another little jab.'